Fit Girls: Exercise is Murder (Large Print Cozy Mystery)

Ann Audree

Everything Journals/Novels

Fit Girls: Exercise is Murder **(Large Print Cozy Mystery)** by Ann Audree is published by Everything Journals/Novels.

© 2019 Everything Novels (Originally published as a Kindle Jan. 9, 2019)

© 2020 Ann Pashak/Everything Novels (Re-published as a Kindle w/new cover)

Cover Artwork licensed through iStock.

Interior decorative breaks licensed through Canva.

ISBN-13: 979-8-9870530-2-7

Contents

Chapter 1

Chased By a Killer

"We have one chance to catch the killer!"

Paisley Summerhill leaned against a cafe table to whisper to her younger friend, Ellie Cruz.

"I'd rather get dessert," Ellie said, having a soft spot for all comfort food after dropping out of college. She looked around the cafe and spotted a dessert cart.

Being ten years older and sensitive to her friend's stress, Paisley didn't want to push. She also didn't want to miss her chance at catching a killer and clearing her name. "Maybe I should do this alone."

"No way!" Ellie forgot her need to feed for a second.

"I don't want to put you in danger," Paisley admitted, "and I'm not too sure I'm ready to face this guy."

"I'm helping. Done deal," Ellie insisted. She crossed her arms, unwilling to retreat. "And if my brother agreed to us acting as bait—"

Dishes clattered from inside the cafe, interrupting. The sound made them both jump, and completely hid the guilty look on Paisley's face.

"It's nothing. Right?" Ellie looked around. "I think we're sticking out because we haven't ordered anything. What do people do when they're in a cafe? Eat."

"Or kiss," Paisley added.

The only other people on the terrace cafe were a waiter cleaning up and two guests cuddling in a dark corner—lovebirds enjoying a nightcap and the lake view. Most guests had already retired after a day of activities and pampering at the Grand Teton

Bluebird Resort. Tucked into the famous Wyoming Teton range, the mountain top getaway specialized in fitness cushioned by expensive luxury.

"We should move this to the boardwalk," Paisley decided, zipping her workout jacket against the evening breeze. "We're not going to lure the killer out of hiding here. Not with witnesses."

"We're not? Good." The olive-skinned cutie let her eyes return to the dessert cart. "We deserve a break. There's only so much mystery a girl can take. Now, that slice of carrot cake is a much better puzzle to solve. Do you think it has enough cream cheese icing to make all those carrots taste good?"

Paisley stepped between Ellie and the treat. "You've been eating better. Don't give up now."

"I have been eating better," Ellie said, taking out her cell phone and lining up a shot of all the desserts. "Now, I get my reward."

Paisley headed toward a short flight of stairs that led from the outdoor patio to a boardwalk circling the pristine lake. She breathed in the evening air, calming her nerves with starlight and fireflies. The moonlight highlighted her ash blonde hair, as she turned back to her almost-sister. "We have to go!"

More interested in taking a selfie with the dessert, Ellie said, "Eating carrots is still eating better."

"Not those carrots!" Paisley hissed, waiting at the top of the stairs. She took a startled step down, when another crash from inside the cafe clattered for attention. A worry line creased her forehead. "What was that?"

"A clumsy waiter about to be fired." Ellie stuck a finger into the carrot cake icing, making a wish that it wouldn't make her sick, like most carbs and dairy lately. They made her whole system rebel.

"Hello... the killer!" Paisley held up her hands in a strangling motion.

It had no effect on Ellie, who savored the delicious flavor in her mouth. Her taste buds overrode all reason. "If I'm going to die, I should get a last wish; and I wish to get a slice to go."

Another ringing crash sounded from inside the cafe. And the lights turned off.

Paisley and Ellie looked around. They were completely alone on the balcony.

"Did you see the couple leave?" Ellie asked. "Or the waiter."

"I was too busy talking to you." Paisley bit her lower lip.

"We're not good at this." Ellie turned to the nearby bushes and waved, raising both hands over her head. The signal was big enough to be seen by bushes on the other side of the lake. "I'm done being bait. Timeout! Hello."

Hurrying back to her friend, Paisley grabbed one arm and tugged toward the outdoor exit. "No one is coming to help us."

"Why not?" Ellie whined, deserting the dessert tray.

Paisley hurried them toward the stairs. "No one knows we're here…"

"You mean, no one knows we're pretending to be bait for a killer?" Ellie would have screamed if she wasn't completely shocked.

"We'll be fine," Paisley said, almost believing it.

Ellie pointed toward the resort. "Shouldn't we run that way? Where there are people?"

"Too far." Paisley headed them down onto the boardwalk.

"My brother's gonna kill you," Ellie muttered.

"I know, but in my defense, I didn't think this would work." Full of regret, Paisley pointed the way they should go. "Scold later, run now!"

Emitting a little yelp, Ellie hurried after her friend. "What have you done?"

With no time to explain, Paisley picked up her pace. Dim lights dotted the wooden walkway, creating a dreamy setting for an evening stroll... or an all-out sprint for safety.

"Head for the dock!" Paisley pointed, keeping her voice as low as possible.

Barely twenty feet long, the wooden pier housed several pontoon boats for resort guests to putter around the lake. Paisley reached it first and scanned the tethered vessels. They were meant for fishing, daytime or night, and seated four to six people under a collapsible canopy. Spotting one named the Rusty Fig, she hurried to its side and cast off all the ropes. "Jump in!"

"Have you gone completely nuts?" Ellie asked, finally reaching the dock, but making no move to get into the boat. She bent over, out of breath. "Please tell me you're doing this to make me exercise?"

"I'm not," Paisley motioned her to hurry, "although regular jogging is a good idea."

Ellie grabbed her side, trying to breathe normally. "You're acting like we're being chased, but I still haven't seen anyone. Could we be overreacting?"

They looked back at the cafe.

Paisley leapt onto the Rusty Fig. "I've got a feeling. Get in the boat."

Ellie wanted to complain, but did as she was told. "You know, I'm not a good swimmer."

"Then don't fall out!" Paisley shoved the boat away from the pier.

The moon ducked behind clouds, shrouding them in an eerie half-light. Rushing to the helm, Paisley collided with the pontoon's captain chair.

"Are you okay?" Ellie heard the collision.

Mumbling to herself, Paisley scrambled into the seat, finding a key in the ignition. "Hold onto something!" She turned the key, but nothing happened. Deadly silence closed in all around.

"I'm still holding." The clouds parted and Ellie could see her friend turning the ignition on and off. "I think you also need to do the Hokey Pokey. Then it should work." She suddenly found their urgency absurd, wondering again if anyone was even following them.

"Guess that's why they left the key in the ignition," Paisley sounded defeated. "The engine's dead."

"Aren't these electric?" Ellie flipped up a seat cushion, exposing a panel. Lifting it, she found the boat's battery with the help of her cell phone light. The connector was detached. Ellie clipped it back into place. "Try again."

Paisley turned the key. Still nothing.

Ellie came to the bow, trying to see around her friend. "Is it in neutral?"

"It's in neutral." Paisley grumbled, noticing that they'd only drifted three feet from the dock. The lake was calm. They'd get nowhere without the engine.

Looking over her shoulder, Paisley squinted at the shadows. There were several long ones where the dock joined the boardwalk. A figure shifted. At least, she thought she saw movement.

Ellie shooed Paisley out of the way. "I'm beginning to think this is a total waste of time, but if you want a midnight cruise, you're gonna get one."

"We aren't alone."

A shadowy figure appeared at the end of the dock—no mistaking it. The clouds shifted, briefly illuminating something shiny in the stranger's hands.

"Who's that?" Ellie's heart instantly picked up its pace.

Paisley pulled her friend into a squat, partially hiding them. She peered over the edge of the craft, hoping the cloud cover would shift again. She needed a little more moonlight to see their pursuer.

"What is he doing? Is it a he?" Ellie couldn't make out the figure at the end of the dock.

The stranger lingered there, blocking any exit by foot.

Paisley counted softly to calm her nerves. "I don't know who it is, and I apologize for getting you into this."

"Just get us out," Ellie begged.

A crackling sound snapped and sparked from the stranger's direction. Ellie squinted, unsure of the noise. "That sounds..." she started to say.

"...bad," Paisley finished. She recognized the sizzling snaps as electrical. "Water and electricity don't mix."

"Oh, good thing we're not near water," Ellie said, as the boat gently bobbed on the lake.

With a little prayer, Paisley tried the ignition key, again. "Please, please..."

If they didn't get away from the dock, they'd be dead in the water... in more ways than one.

49 Hours Earlier or in Fit Girls' Time...

- 8 kickboxing classes

- 5 spin classes

- 6 aqua-aerobics sessions

- 11 private consultations

- 1 mountain hike

- a jog around the lake... oh, and... one less dead body.

Gasping for air and everyone's attention, Mr. Felix Newton collapsed on the floor.

"Sir, you aren't dying." Practical and athletic, Paisley Summerhill stood over the prostrate, chubby form of her most challenging guest. She pasted on a smile.

"You're killing me!" he sobbed in an ear-pleasing Australian accent that didn't take any of the venom out of his words.

Kneeling next to him, Paisley patted his arm. "I know how you feel," she said, remembering her own fear of trying something new. Of course, her fear was about a much bigger commitment than losing a few pounds. "Maybe you'd feel better starting with a beginner class instead of my advanced spin class."

"A beginner's class?" he spewed out the words like they were an insult.

The whir of ten stationary bikes filled the workout room at the Grand Teton Bluebird Resort, a little piece of pampered heaven hidden among the pine trees. Sympathetic eyes quickly looked away, as the other guests hunkered down and peddled like maniacs.

One cycler took a bit longer to turn away: a stylish woman in her forties, wearing a pink workout suit. She offered them a wistful look, before focusing on her pedaling.

As a visiting fitness trainer, Paisley hadn't been at the resort long enough to make any friends or earn the respect she'd had at her last job. The staff was nice but distant. The aloof management hadn't even welcomed her yet. The only upside had been the guests' support. Their turnout, over her first two days on the job, had created a buzz that filled up the rest of her classes. With things shifting her way, Paisley dreaded a setback. She couldn't afford an unhappy customer. Mr. Newton's temper tantrum could easily turn into a firestorm of resort gossip. Paisley had to act fast.

"I know exactly what you need." She grabbed a water bottle, setting it on the floor next to Mr. Newton's heaving chest. "You need a bigger challenge. Hydrate, please."

He peeked an eye in her direction.

Absently tugging on her long, ash-blonde ponytail, Paisley considered how to handle the situation. Newton probably needed a swift kick in his ample derriere; however, she preferred to inspire her clients toward success... whatever amount they were capable of achieving. Plus, taking a power position rarely worked with ambitious, wealthy men.

"I apologize, Mr. Newton," she said, relieved to see him sit up and listen. "I've seen this before. An adventurous outdoorsman like yourself can't be cooped up inside on a stationary bike. You require more from your exercise. I have one spot left in tomorrow morning's Hiking Class. We take a strenuous path, but the views are to die for. You can use your cell phone, but if you have a camera you should bring it along to take pictures."

Mr. Newton grumbled something that sounded like "yes." Struggling to his feet, he scanned the room and pointed his chin in the air. "Spin class. Bah!"

As he lumbered out of the room, Paisley wanted to chase after him and ask if she should expect him for the hike. He certainly needed some kind of exercise. She couldn't help but notice that his skin had an unhealthy tinge.

"Three more minutes," Paisley called out to her spinners, turning to stare out a massive picture window.

The training room had a spectacular view of the valley with all the bikes and treadmills pointed at the window. Paisley pretended to take in the vista, but she really needed a minute to compose herself. Unfortunately, all she could see were the waving hands of Mr. Newton. Like a little tornado of destruction, he hurried toward a woman wearing a Grand Teton Bluebird Resort uniform—a tailored crimson blazer with sleek black slacks. It hugged her feminine body in all the right places, which couldn't be said for all employee uniforms.

Paisley decided it must have been tailored to fit so well, which was a smart move. She also surmised that the stylish woman was her new boss, general manager Felicity Lange. She'd heard rumors about the raven-haired woman. They warned of strict rules and no second chances. Even though employee gossip usually held a kernel of truth, Paisley still hated to give it too much credence. She'd rather make up her own mind about Loggerhead Lange's harsh reputation, and if her iron fist would really oust any employee who tainted the resort's five-star rating.

The manager listened intently to Mr. Newton, eyes shifting up the hill to spot Paisley at the window. The glare was far from welcoming, and came across as a silent summons.

"Great class, Miss Summerhill," the stylish woman in the pink workout suit said, as she patted her face with a towel. "I look forward to taking another one tomorrow."

"Hopefully, I'll still be here." Paisley hardly looked at the woman, although it wasn't difficult to ignore her cologne. Not many people sprayed expensive perfume on themselves before a workout. To Paisley, it smelled like flowery urine. She assumed her nose, at least the smelling part, was broken. She let it go, closing up the training room and heading out to meet her new boss.

Chapter 2

Everyone's a Suspect

"The guest is always right," Felicity Lange lectured her new fitness instructor, as they headed along one of the many paths that crisscrossed the resort's property. "Mr. Newton, however, is a pest. Adorable, at times, but complaining is his hobby. Don't let it bother you."

Majestic pine trees towered above them, making Paisley feel even smaller. She tried to keep up with Felicity, but the manager's long stride kept her half a step ahead. She briefly glanced back. A disapproving frown seemed to negate all her reassuring words.

"Did he mention the hike?" Paisley asked, hoping her solution to Mr. Newton's exercise regime might impress her new boss. "I'm wondering if I should offer him an option to the morning hike, like maybe a private water aerobics class?"

"He didn't say," Felicity grumbled, "but he certainly snapped up a free mud bath when I offered it."

The resort's mud baths were legendary. Heated by an underground aquifer, they maintained a steamy one hundred-degree temperature and were known to heal aches and pains. At least, the resort's brochure raved about the mud's healing properties.

"Why don't you pop over to the mudroom and give him the option?" Felicity suggested. "It's the least you can do to smooth things over a bit." Felicity stopped suddenly, causing Paisley to bump into her.

"Sorry," she said quickly, looking down. For a brief second, she saw a silver heart attached to a linked bracelet on Felicity's wrist.

The general manager took a deep breath, standing her ground. A linebacker wouldn't have been able to take her out. "Mr. Newton is a unique breed of guest," she said. "We specialize in his kind of uniqueness. Show me you know how to take care of our most special clientele, and you'll have a long future at the Grand Teton Bluebird Resort."

Apologizing did not come easy for Paisley. She knew groveling was expected of her, but she needed help. Before heading over to find the most disagreeable Mr. Newton, she tracked down Ellie and persuaded her to tag along.

"I'm just saying," Ellie shrugged, as she followed Paisley through the main resort building's hallway, "it's a long, stupid name for a resort. Can't we just call it the Bluebird?"

Paisley shook her head. She didn't care about the resort's name. "I need Felicity's glowing recommendation, so I can extend this experiment to other high-end resorts."

Ellie chuckled. "Is that what we're calling it—an experiment? I thought you were running away from the altar."

"And how is that diet coming?" Paisley asked, shifting the topic from something she didn't want to talk about to something her friend would rather ignore.

"Okay, I'll shut up about the resort's name and your need for temporary work far away from a certain man." Ellie sniffed like she had a lot more to say on the subject but let it drop. "Speaking of my brother, are you ever going to call him?"

"Are you?" Paisley countered.

"I'll take that as a no." Ellie swung her arms, pulling the right one up to show off her muscle. Or lack of one. "That's two days of weight training, baby."

Paisley finally allowed herself a smile. "You are amazing. Did Chef Armand have any gluten-free options for your meals?"

"Yes, but come on, I can't go gluten-free," Ellie complained. "Can't I just go veggie-free?"

Taking it as a joke, Paisley shook her head. She didn't want to push too hard. Ellie went through a lot when her health interfered with her second year at college. "You'll feel better, you'll have more energy... just about everything will be better once you shift to a completely gluten-free diet."

"I'm pretty sure my tastebuds will revolt," Ellie said.

"Don't worry," Paisley said, taking her arm, as they pushed through double doors leading outside. "I'll get your body back in balance, including your tastebuds. They just need to learn there's more to food than carbs and sugar."

Ellie brightened. "The good news... Chef Armie is yummie, and I do mean that in a hunk-a-licious way; although he did mention something about a tasty way to cook lotus roots. No one's perfect. Luckily, I found it easy to listen by watching his lips move. I think I'm in love. Is it okay to fraternize with the help?"

They broke into the sunlight, following a well worn path. At a fork, a little collection of wooden signs pointed to various spots—the hot springs pool, the dock and the mud baths. They followed the one pointing down a winding path to mud therapy.

"Will it smell?" Ellie asked, already preparing for the worse. "I've never really cared for wet dirt."

"It's not a pig pen," Paisley said, well versed in mud bath benefits. "It's a combination of volcanic ash, peat moss and boiling spring water. Sometimes, they add a scent like lavender or eucalyptus."

Ellie playfully nudged her arm. "Did you write the brochure or something?"

"I love mud baths," Paisley said, a little offended. "They open your pores and pull out toxins."

"Maybe I could dip in a toe, while you make nice with Mr. Awful?"

Paisley assumed all the mud baths would be full but didn't want to crush Ellie's hopes. "There they are," she pointed.

At the end of the path, a collection of wedge-shaped buildings surrounded an inner gazebo. Each wedge had a steamed-up glass door and canvas roof. A halo of steam swirled upward from each tiny structure, slowly releasing the heat within. Soothing New Age music completed the perfect retreat.

The gazebo housed a Bluebird employee with a supply of towels and water bottles. "Are you checking in for your mud bath?" she asked. Her name tag read: Vicki.

"Can we just peek at one?" Ellie wanted to know.

"Not right now," Vicki explained. "They're all full."

Ellie pouted. "I thought there would be more of them or a big pool of mud for volleyball or something."

"No such luck," the girl said, seeming to like the idea. "They're all private mud baths, although they are big enough for couples." She looked at the friends like they might want to share one.

"No, I work here," Paisley explained.

"We have a hard enough time sharing a hotel room," Ellie giggled. It elicited a similar sound from the mud bath attendant.

Before Ellie could worm her way into a hut for a quick peek, Paisley interrupted, "I need to check on Mr. Newton. Which one is he in?"

The girl pointed behind them. "He's over his time," the girl frowned. "Could you hurry him along?"

Paisley nodded, waving at Ellie to hang back. She didn't need an audience while she ate humble pie.

Knocking on the glass door, she listened for a response. Hearing nothing, she opened the door a crack. "It's Paisley Summerhill, can I come in?"

All she heard was the soft bubbling of hot mud. The scent of eucalyptus covered up some of the earthy smell. Paisley pushed the door open enough to stick her head inside. "Are you decent? Oh! Mr. Newton!" she exclaimed, quickly retreating from the door.

"What's wrong?" Ellie came up behind her, along with the teenage attendant.

Paisley turned a stunned face to them. "I just made it worse."

"What did you see?" Ellie wanted all the dirty details.

"All I saw was skin." Paisley made a face.

The teenage attendant snorted. "Happens all the time." She knocked on the glass door. "Mr. Newton, time's up." They heard movement inside. "See? They want you to catch them getting dressed."

"Gross." It was Ellie's turn to make a face. "Haven't they heard of MeToo?"

A muffled groan vibrated in a weird way from the other side of the glass door. Paisley looked up, hearing the noise more through the canvas roof above. She pushed the attendant out of the way and rushed into the room.

Mr. Newton was up to his neck in the mud bath, except for one arm hanging out of the tub. His head lolled backwards, eyes wide open with a blank stare. Paisley ran to him, feeling for a pulse, but she knew Mr. Newton wouldn't be complaining to anyone ever again.

As coroner assistants moved the body, Paisley, Ellie and attendant Vicki waited in an adjacent mudroom. All the other guests had been taken back to the main building to be questioned. Paisley peeked out the door, which she'd insisted be left open. Her excuse was the heat. Even without getting into the mud bath, the rooms were steamy hot. They were natural saunas; however, she really wanted the door open so she could snoop.

Paisley leaned forward from her spot on the edge of the mud bath. She could see through the door crack and studied the police officers controlling the crime scene. Their eyes drifted her way every so often. "I'm going to ask someone," she said, making up her mind.

"No!" Ellie snapped. "Weren't you like one of the last people to see him alive? Or at least part of him? They might think you did it."

The thought hadn't occurred to Paisley. She frowned, turned to Vicki, who slowly ripped the label off a water bottle. "What was Mr. Newton like when he came in?"

The girl narrowed her eyes at Paisley. "The usual."

"You knew him?" Paisley asked, surprised.

The girl shrugged. "Everyone knows him. He's a regular. Comes to Bluebird every other month or so to torture us."

Paisley and Ellie shared a look. The mud attendant saw it. "Hey!" she raised her voice. "I didn't do anything. It's not my fault!"

"How long did he go over his time in the mud bath?" Paisley asked, instantly regretting how it sounded like an accusation. "I mean... Mr. Newton was clearly a difficult guest, with a history of pulling his birthday suit trick on you. No wonder you sent me to check on him."

The mud attendant jumped to her feet. "Are you saying he died because I let him stay in the mud bath too long? Take it back!"

Paisley bit her lip.

Ellie stood up, too, moving to a spot between the women. "Let's lower our voices. We don't want to worry the nice police officers."

"Maybe I do," Vicki said, but she lowered her voice.

"My friend just likes to ask questions," Ellie explained. "No one is saying anything about anybody." Her last words were directed at Paisley with a what-the-heck-are-you-starting look.

"I would never hurt him!" Vicki insisted. "He's a great tipper! At least, he was."

Ellie rubbed her right ear, giving it a little massage. Vicki's explosive rant was rather ear piercing. "That makes sense." She hoped agreeing would sooth the girl's indignation.

Paisley, however, had other such plans. "Let me get this straight. Mr. Newton was your cash cow, so you resented his tricks but put up with them because of the money?"

"You make it sound like I was the only one who benefited," Vicki spat out with a huff. "Do you know how much he spends here? Management named a boat after him, they loved him that much. Just ask Marika in the gift shop. She always stocks the bling when he makes a reservation."

The thought of any woman looking forward to a gift from Mr. Newton turned Paisley's stomach. "You forget that I met the man. No amount of money or expensive gifts would have made me like him."

"Hmm... now who sounds like they wanted him dead?" Vicki stalked out of the mudroom, heading for the nearest police officer.

Ellie retreated to a bench. "Your people skills are really lacking today."

"I couldn't agree more." Paisley pinched a pressure point on her shoulder. It didn't release any of the tension she felt.

"I kinda bought her excuse," Ellie said. "That was some conviction, you know? That scream... my right ear still doesn't feel normal."

Paisley saw it differently. "She sounded very local theater to me."

Catching the last part, Vicki snorted as she returned with a trooper. "She did it!" The damning declaration came with a sneer for Paisley.

"What's going on?" the twenty-something officer acted like he'd already lived three lives and had seen it all. "I'm Trooper Agnew. Do we have a problem here?"

"She gave Mr. Newton a brutal workout just before his mud bath," Vicki shouted. A finger of accusation stabbed in Paisley's direction. "She killed Mr. Newton!"

Two more officers turned in their direction.

Ellie closed her eyes, mortified.

"That's right," the mud attendant huffed, "Mr. Newton told me all about how she worked him to death in her spin class. He begged her to stop, but it wasn't until he fell to the floor that he was able to escape."

Agnew crossed his arms. A put-upon wrinkle creased his brow. Every move he made seemed to send an intimidating message. Not hard to do, considering his broad shoulders and muscular body could pack a punch. His steely attention turned to Paisley. "Was Mr. Newton in your spin class?" he asked, assessing her with a quick once over.

"Mr. Newton was in my spin class for all of five minutes," Paisley launched into an explanation, barely stopping to breathe. "He complained for three of them, got on the stationary bike, pushed the pedal once, then stumbled off and dramatically fell to the floor."

Ellie licked her lips, a nervous tick she'd fallen into as a child. Today, it was more warranted. She stood again, putting a hand on her friend's arm in hopes of calming her down. It didn't work.

"Get the facts straight before you accuse people of murder," Paisley snapped at the mud attendant.

"You accused me first!" the girl countered, tears coming to her eyes.

"No, I didn't, you jumped to a conclusion," Paisley corrected. "It's a fact that you asked me to check on Mr. Newton when it was your job. Were you just lazy or did you have a reason?"

Vicki turned to the trooper, her big eyes blinked. "Are you gonna let her talk to me like that?"

His stern look didn't soften. "Yes. Answer the question."

Ellie edged closer to Paisley and whispered in a singsong voice, "You still have to work here."

Vicki scrunched up her nose. She'd clearly be spreading some Paisley gossip. "I'd rather wait until Ms. Lange arrives. She's the resort—"

"I know who she is," Agnew interrupted. "She's a local, like me. I happen to know she's not your mom or your legal guardian. She doesn't even like kids. Answer the question."

Trapped by his authority, Vicki had no choice but to answer. "Mr. Newton could be difficult, so sure, I let her check on him, but I didn't kill him!"

"Wasn't he overweight?" Ellie interjected. "He probably died of natural causes."

"Which wouldn't be my fault!" Vicki exclaimed.

"Right, no foul play here... for anyone," Ellie chimed in, making every effort to shift the conversation away from blaming Vicki or Paisley of murder. "We certainly don't need to use the M-word."

"Yes, we do," Paisley said at the same time Trooper Agnew said, "No, we don't."

For a moment, his rough exterior cracked. Not in a good way. His handsome scowl turned into a sneer. "Who are you, again?" he asked, genuinely annoyed.

"We're only here for a short engagement. A three month long engagement. I'm gonna stop saying engagement now." Ellie instantly shut her mouth.

Agnew silenced her with one look.

"Mr. Newton had scorch marks on his face," Paisley said, ignoring the officer's question and his baffled expression.

His eyebrows rose, looking toward Newton's mudroom. "Scorch marks?"

"He had a gray mark on his left cheek, plus others on his chin and ear." Paisley said, matter of fact.

"Thank you, Nancy Drew," Vicki muttered.

Paisley sensed Vicki was itching for a fight. She knew it was her fault. The girl's actions shouldn't have bothered her so much, but her defenses were up. The last couple of months were to blame, not Vicki. Paisley would have to make amends. For now, however, it seemed wiser to help Agnew. "Have you ever heard of Tough Mudder?"

"Yes, and I saw the marks," Agnew acknowledged. "They looked like mud."

"I did a Tough Mudder race last year, and one of the obstacles was crawling under a live wire."

"On purpose?" Ellie scoffed.

"What happened?" the trooper asked, his curiosity building. "Did anyone die?"

Paisley shook her head. "No, the voltage was low because they knew some runners would get shocked; however, the mud got a little wetter than planned, and it got dangerous. The water gave the shock more power. No one died, but several members of my team came away with nasty burns that marked them with the same gray tinge. Just like Mr. Newton."

"Are the tubs hooked up to any kind of electricity?" Agnew asked Vicki. "Maybe for cleaning?"

"Are you nuts?" Vicki asked, before realizing she was talking to a police officer. "I mean, no. It's mud. You don't clean mud."

"The tubs are made of concrete," an authoritative female voice cut through Vicki's apology. The resort manager had arrived. "Trooper Agnew, I'm glad to see our tragedy in capable hands. How have you been?"

His demeanor softened. "Better than your guest."

"I'd really like to move all my employees out of this area," she said. It wasn't an order, but she made it sound like an obvious choice. "I offer you our conference room for taking statements, and our usual stunning accommodations for everyone to wait."

"Fine." Agnew seemed happy to leave them for the moment.

While Felicity shot a pointed look at Vicki to make a hasty retreat, she gave her newest employee—Paisley—no further notice. Ellie took her friend by the arm and led her away; however, she couldn't stop Paisley from slowing down as they passed by the crime scene.

"Look," Paisley whispered, noticing as an officer put a to-go soda-sized cup into an evidence bag. "What was Newton drinking?"

"Let it go," Ellie hissed.

On the winding path back to the main resort building, they kept their own counsel until they were far enough away not to be overheard. Paisley let out a sigh. She dared to look back over her shoulder at the way they had come.

"Way to go," Ellie said to her friend, believing she'd just destroyed her reputation at the Grand Teton Bluebird Resort. "You turned Vicki into a ballistic missile who will try to sink your career."

"Well, it's better than letting her spread rumors that I caused a guest's death," Paisley replied, although, it didn't make her feel better.

"I'm just saying... the staff here seems close-knit." Ellie shrugged.

"At least Trooper Agnew listened to me." Paisley had to take the win. It might be the only one she would get.

Ellie laughed, reading a little more into her friend's words. "You're too old for him."

The matter-of-fact statement hit Paisley like a slap. "If you have to say something like that, you should say that he's too young for me." Paisley corrected the error. "It makes it sound a little less like I'm about to shrivel up and die."

"He's too young for you," Ellie said with a smile as big as Lewis Carroll's Cheshire Cat.

"Last I checked, life begins at thirty," Paisley said, thinking it over. "Isn't thirty the new twenty-five?"

Ellie shook her head. "I never said you were old. Geez, what will you be like at forty?"

"Forty!" Paisley couldn't think that far ahead.

"I take it back!" Ellie decided.

Paisley watched the path for rough spots. "The last few hours have been a disaster, and I don't see how it could get any worse."

A siren whined from the resort's main drive, casting blue and red lights upward against the pine trees. The sound cut off abruptly.

"More police?" Paisley asked. Her heart stopped, as they came around the curved path to the front of the resort. Waiting for them was a U.S. Marshal's car, with an agent leaning against the hood.

Ellie gasped. "It just got worse."

Grabbing Ellie's arm, Paisley turned them toward the main entrance. "We need to disappear."

Their escape, however, caught the attention of the U.S. Marshal in question. He pushed away from his car and stuck two fingers in his mouth. The shrill whistle stopped Paisley and Ellie from disappearing into the resort.

"This is not happening." Paisley braced herself.

"Oh, I think it is," Ellie said. "Whatever you do, don't mention the thing."

Paisley sighed. "The thing?"

"The wedding thing."

Paisley could have died on the spot.

Chapter 3

Chasing Clues

Deputy Marshal Dolan Cruz wore a quizzical look. He was clearly happy to see Paisley and Ellie alive and well, but he hesitated a moment too long. Pushing away from the official U.S. Marshal sedan, he opened his arms in welcome. A knowing smirk took over his rugged face. Stubble marked his olive skin but only added to the pleasing shape of his lean, dark features. The suit helped too, as well as the Deputy Marshal badge showing on his belt when the wind blew his jacket open.

"What is he doing here?" Paisley whispered to Ellie.

"Being protective." She frowned but gave her brother a little wave.

Paisley pulled her long hair to the side, letting the afternoon's gentle breeze reach her neck. "We just found the body, and it's over three hours to his office in Cheyenne."

"Okay, he's being overprotective," Ellie said, "but I wouldn't lead with that."

They barely reached Dolan when Trooper Agnew rushed up, having apparently ran all the way from mud therapy. "Welcome to Juniper County, sir. We don't get many U.S. Marshals up here." Agnew almost sounded territorial.

"You must be chasing a fugitive or something, right? Just happen to be in the area?" Ellie asked, once again trying to smooth over an awkward moment.

Dolan still had an arm out, and Ellie stepped close for a quick hug. Paisley shifted uneasily, making no move to follow suit.

Agnew took it all in, and nodded as if he were taking mental notes. "You seem to know two of our witnesses." He briefed Dolan on the limited facts, pointing out that Paisley and Ellie discovered the body. "Of course, these ladies are potential suspects."

"I can vouch for them until the evidence proves they're only witnesses," Dolan said, pointedly turning to Paisley. "They were just in the wrong place at the wrong time."

"You're welcome," she said.

Dolan let it slide, continuing to address the trooper like a lackey. "You can turn your investigation toward the mudroom attendant and Newton's wife."

"Sir?" Agnew riled a bit at the tone. "Around here, we prefer to question our witnesses and eliminate suspects the old fashioned way—with evidence."

"Just saving time, trooper. Evidence tends to grow cold when you waste it on false leads." Dolan pointed to Ellie. "That one's my little sister, and that one..." but he couldn't finish the sentence. He didn't have a simple label for Paisley.

"Nothing. I'm his nothing." Paisley put on a big smile. Too big.

"Anymore." Dolan looked a little uneasy.

"She was something," Ellie blurted out. "Now she's not."

"I think he gets it," Dolan said.

"Everyone gets it," Paisley mumbled.

Agnew indulged in his first smile of the day, taking a moment to consult his notepad.

Ellie scrunched up her nose, realizing she hadn't helped at all. "You really think we're suspects?" she asked the trooper.

Paisley half-turned to Agnew, "You can treat me like a suspect. I'm confident that you'll eliminate me and move on."

Her eyes angled toward Dolan.

"I'm only here to consult," Dolan promised, although his tone said otherwise. "I do have a few questions, though. Can you round up the resort manager?"

"Do you order everyone around?" Paisley bristled. "Or just anyone wearing uniforms?"

Her defense produced Agnew's second smile of the day, perhaps of his life. He did not give the impression that he even liked to smile.

Dolan saw it and instantly repeated his request which sent Agnew away. "Don't flirt with the officers. Either of you. They're busy."

Ellie quickly stepped between Paisley and Dolan, playfully punching her brother in the arm. "You didn't have to swoop in and rescue us."

He disagreed. "Didn't I? What would you do, if you heard your family had found a dead body?"

Paisley flinched at the word 'family.'

"First, I'd wonder how I accidentally followed my sister, when I clearly should be miles and miles away at home." Ellie's dimples softened her accusation.

"What really happened?" Dolan asked, ignoring any wrongdoing.

Neither of the women jumped to answer. "So, you're not leaving this to the locals?" Ellie asked.

Dolan shook his head. "No way," he said, taking a little pleasure from the stunned looks on their faces. "Once the U.S. Marshal's department is interested in a case, we follow it to the end. I'll be staying for the duration."

Paisley nodded, holding her chin up and squaring her shoulders. "It'll be just like the honeymoon we never had."

Dolan took Paisley's elbow and led her a couple of steps away from his sister.

She shot a help-me look over her shoulder, but Ellie only shrugged unable to cross that line and wallow in her brother's love life, at least not right in front of his face.

"I'm sorry if my presence disrupts your flirting," Dolan said, eyes narrowing.

"I don't flirt," Paisley said.

"Well, the object of your desire is barely twenty-one," Dolan's harsh whisper suggested that she might catch a disease. "At the very least, you're ten years older than Trooper Agnew."

The direct hit made Paisley suck in a breath. Even if she didn't look her age, she didn't want to be limited by a date on a calendar. "You can stop worrying about my love life. It's not your problem anymore."

He leaned his head toward hers. "I'm glad you said it first," he admitted, "you're love life is a problem."

Paisley jerked her arm out of his grasp. "I can talk to men without wanting to date them."

"Can I rejoin the conversation," Ellie asked, "or are we gonna keep pretending I can't hear you?"

"We're done," Paisley said, having every intention of avoiding Dolan for the rest of his time at the Grand Teton Bluebird Resort.

"I agree with Agnew about one thing," Dolan said. "You're a suspect, Paisley, and after I settle in, I'll need to take your statement and have you walk me through the crime scene. That is, if you're right and Newton was killed."

Paisley looked forward to proving she was right. In fact, she decided to solve the whole case for him. It would be the perfect revenge.

A heavy silence hung over the Grand Teton Bluebird Resort, no more so than in Paisley Summerhill's hotel room.

Paisley slid open the balcony door, letting in the sweet smell of pine. It helped to erase the scent of death lingering in her hair. In spite of a shower and changing her clothes, she could still smell it. Perhaps it was locked in her memory; but it hadn't been the first time she'd seen a dead body, just the first time that she'd been closely involved.

"Are you going to bed early?" she asked Ellie, who had also showered and changed.

Ellie pulled the queen-sized bed covers up to her nose. She made no effort to get up. Instead, she growled like a bear caught in a trap. "You need to fix it."

"Maybe you should order room service," Paisley suggested.

"It was mean and that's not like you." Ellie threw back the covers. She was fully dressed, wearing jeans and a light-weight, pink flannel top. She looked down at her shirt and smoothed out the front, trying to stretch out the wrinkles. "I know he seems like a tough guy, but he has feelings. Maybe, just maybe, he came here to finally explain things to you."

Paisley turned her back on the view. "I'm going to check out the gift shop, then I'll head to dinner."

Ellie jumped up. She groaned, unable to tell what her friend was really up to with her plans.

"You want to come with, or meet me in the dining room?" Paisley asked.

"Wouldn't I be in the way? You might want to seek out Officer Agnew and flirt." Ellie reverted for a moment to her teenage years. She had a tendency for the dramatic in high school.

With an indulging laugh, Paisley headed to the door. "I doubt I'll ever flirt again, but I did make him smile—"

"See!"

"—which means, he'll probably talk to me if my one little clue leads to something." Paisley grabbed a leather jacket off the chair.

"That's still flirting," Ellie said. "And it's mean to do it in front of Dolan."

"You know what's mean?" Paisley countered. "Leaving someone at the altar!"

She exited the room, shutting the door with a solid thud.

Ellie scrunched up her nose, and fell back on the bed. "You don't have to be right all the time. It's annoying."

The gift store clerk, Marika, greeted Paisley with a sad smile. Age had turned her hair gray, but it suited her oval face and blue eyes. "Everything is on sale this week," she said, a slight Russian accent marked her speech, making the resort seem very international.

Paisley quickly explained who she was and her interest in Mr. Newton. "I know you might not want to talk to me, but I have a vested interest. I found his body."

With a little sniff, Marika quickly grabbed a tissue. "Oh, dear, please excuse me."

Paisley couldn't help but notice the woman's puffy eyes and redness around her nose. "No, I'm sorry. Sometimes I'm a little too direct. Did you know Mr. Newton?"

Marika pulled out two trays of glittering jewelry. "His passing is why everything is on sale." She reached behind her to turn on a fan. "Is it just me or is it hot in here?"

"I'm fine," Paisley said, but the little fan stirred up the air around them. Paisley's nose involuntarily wrinkled in response. She caught a hint of a familiar smell. The same stinky perfume she'd noticed on the workout lady was also the brand Marika used. Clearly, I'm the only one that thinks it smells bad, Paisley thought.

Taking a step sideways to avoid the fan's airflow, she checked out the jewelry selection. Paisley marveled at the choices. She couldn't believe it was all bought with Mr. Newton in mind. A resort gift shop was hardly the best place to purchase gems. She voiced as much, admiring pea-sized diamond studs.

"Only the best, at the best price," Marika said. "Our Mr. Newton was a haggler."

Whatever he was, he wasn't cheap, Paisley thought. She fingered a necklace with a stunning tear drop diamond. "That's quite a selection to stock for one man."

"I suppose it was a risk," the business woman said. "I can't believe he's gone."

Paisley realized she wasn't just sad about losing a customer. She'd lost something more. "I'm surprised you are at work. It seems like you lost a friend."

The woman tucked her tissue away, shaking her head like she wanted to disagree. "I'm only thinking of myself, I know, but I never realized how much I needed him. For business."

Paisley looked up from the jewelry. An eyebrow naturally rose.

"I mean... he was a good customer, and now I have all this stock. It will take a good six months or longer to sell it all now."

Paisley admired one of five identical silver bracelets on the tray. Each had one charm attached to the links—a heart. It reminded her of the one she'd seen Felicity wearing. "Wow, his wife was spoiled—in a good way. Although, it is a lot for one woman to wear."

Marika made a noncommittal noise, accompanied by a shrug. Paisley had a sudden thought and instantly blurted it out: "Mr. Newton had a mistress?"

The older lady grabbed the first tray and put it back out of sight. "We don't discuss such things."

It was all the confirmation Paisley needed. Although she had to believe that Mr. Newton came to the resort to hookup, she kept the assumption to herself. "Of course, speculation is totally inappropriate. I just wonder if the police know."

The owner bit her lip, putting the second tray out of sight, as well. She crossed her arms over an ample chest. "Will there be anything else?"

Paisley couldn't help but notice the woman wore a silver bracelet with a heart charm. However, her charm was encrusted with tiny diamonds. Her version was a step above the other ones on the tray. Marika noticed Paisley's stare and quickly tugged her sleeve down to hide the bobble.

"Marika," Paisley leaned into the counter, conspiratorially, "I can see you cared about Mr. Newton. You need to help the police. Frankly, I'm concerned they don't have many leads."

"Not even with forensics?" the shop owner moaned. "How can that be?"

Paisley nodded, making it seem like the police had nothing to go on. Swallowing any remorse for misleading the lady, she said, "They don't have much to work with. The body was in mud."

The gossip did the trick. Marika leaned on the counter, and lowered her voice. "I heard you know that U.S. Marshal."

"Oh, I do, and he is completely frustrated." Paisley nodded, sadly, certain she wasn't lying about Dolan's temperament. He'd certainly be frustrated when he learned she was investigating the murder. "Outside of getting justice for poor Mr. Newton, think of what an unsolved murder will do to the resort? We could all be out of work soon."

"No!" The shop owner looked around at her livelihood. Tears welled in her eyes. "How could this have happened to Newty?"

'Newty?' Paisley wondered just how friendly Marika had been with the billionaire. Maybe her bracelet was a gift, not an advertisement. She considered the woman with new eyes. 'Her tears are heartfelt. That can't just be for her situation with the store and a lost friend. She's heartbroken.' Paisley knew how that felt.

Marika reached for more tissues.

"That's why we need to help," Paisley coaxed. "There's things you and I know that the police could never find out. Am I right?"

Marika nodded. "Newty had a way of talking to people. I loved his voice." She pulled back her sleeve and showed off her bracelet. "He gave his heart—at least as a heart charm—for a first tryst. Beyond that he liked diamonds."

Paisley listened, making all the proper sounds that she understood the attraction, instead of being completely repulsed. "You and Mr. Newton?"

The shop owner waved it off like their union was a thing of the past. "It was early days, and both of us were a lot younger and slimmer." She chuckled at her extra pounds, although she wore them well. "I warned him not to let it get out of hand. I really did."

"How many women were there?" Paisley almost hated to ask.

Marika shrugged. She had no idea. "Newty loved ladies. I always understood, but not everyone is so... European. I worried about jealous husbands, let me tell you. He'd always laugh and say that no one came to the Grand Teton Bluebird Resort to sleep with their wife."

"But... he's married." Paisley felt sorry for his widow.

Marika shrugged again. "I was blinded by love."

Paisley realized there was more to Mr. Newton than she'd seen. He had a dashing side that he backed up with jewelry and a sexy accent. Perhaps he was able to seduce several women at the same time and still keep his wife happy. "Don't you worry, Marika. I'm certain his killer is still at the resort and I'm going to find him!"

Chapter 4

Eating & Accusations

"**A**re you completely nuts!" Ellie screeched, learning of Paisley's new clue.

Her voiced echoed around the Grand Teton Bluebird Resort lobby. The high ceiling spanned three stories with upper hallways open to the view of a massive river rock fireplace on one side and glass windows on the other. They made for an impressive panorama of the alpine setting and a distant waterfall.

Paisley pulled Ellie toward the roaring fire, hoping to keep her from creating a scene. She'd already noticed eyes following them as they crossed the lobby. The rumor mill was definitely up and running.

"You had to go ruin it." Ellie would much rather think about dinner than Mr. Newton's romantic trysts.

"I ruined your appetite?" Paisley asked, glad for the heat of the fireplace in spite of her jacket. She found the spring weather ideal during the day but a tad too cool at night. "I hear food and murder go very well together. Haven't you ever wanted to go to a murder mystery dinner?"

"Not one with a real murder!" Ellie shook her head. "I'm worried about you."

Paisley ignored the concern. "I'm going to solve this murder before Dolan."

Ellie shook her head. "Chef Armand promised he'd make a gluten free dinner that wouldn't make me cry or throw up. Now all I'll be able to think about is Newton scoping out his next conquest in the resort's dining hall."

"You have a point," Paisley admitted. "We should see who else is wearing a silver heart bracelet. Felicity Lange had one."

"Ew." Ellie headed for the dining room. "And I suppose no one could buy one for herself?"

Paisley ignored the question. They walked in silence, until they spotted Dolan leaning against a towering, rough-hewn log pillar. Clearly, he'd been waiting for them, making it impossible to enter the dining room without passing by.

"We need to talk," he said, crooking his finger at Paisley.

"Ellie needs to eat," she countered, "so can we do this over dinner?"

Dolan pulled up short, hearing something in the casual invitation. "You're asking me to dinner?"

Did she? Paisley bit her lower lip. "Uh, not exactly. I mean, not like that."

Dolan grunted, letting go of whatever he thought he heard. "Can't anyway. Still interviewing guests and employees, but did you make a girl in the gift shop cry?"

Ellie hummed a little doomsday tune.

"I was comforting her," Paisley said, unwilling to admit anything damaging. It didn't help.

"Stop it," he ordered. "Stick to doing your job and let me do mine. You are still a fitness instructor, right?"

"I didn't do anything."

"You questioned the mudroom attendant before a police officer and now the gift shop girl?" Dolan wasn't buying it. "Which means we now have to question the gift shop girl."

"Her name is Marika," Paisley offered.

Ellie closed her eyes, wanting to dart away but oddly mesmerized by their tiny battle of wills.

Seeing her friend's distress, Paisley turned up the charm, aiming the full force at Dolan. "Everyone's talking about the death, so it's not really my fault that it comes up. I have to get out there and talk to people to promote my classes. There seems to be a nasty rumor that my training can kill people."

Dolan smiled at his sister, also noting her angst. "And clearly that is a problem, yet, your goodwill campaign feels like a fishing expedition."

"I'm not a child," Ellie said, tired of listening to their super-sweet argument. "Yes, Paisley is investigating Newton's murder."

"Aha!" Dolan jabbed a finger in the air.

"And, clearly, Dolan is too dumb to ask what Paisley has learned," Ellie finished. "Now, I'm going to dinner."

As Ellie stalked off, Dolan gently grabbed Paisley's arm. "What did you learn?"

"I'm sure you would have stumbled across it eventually," Paisley said, sweetly. "Mr. Newton had several lovers. Here. At the resort. At the same time."

Dolan let go of her arm, more interested than he wanted to show.

"Yup," Paisley said, "your pool of suspects just exploded!"

Paisley and Ellie took a table near windows that overlooked the pristine lake. Several guests whispered in their direction.

"It's starting already," Ellie said, keeping her voice low.

"I noticed a few gawkers in the lobby," Paisley admitted. "However, most of them probably only know that we found the body."

"Oh, goody. How long will it take for them to hear he hated your class?" Ellie put on a fake smile and nodded to an older couple sitting nearby. "Evening!"

"What are you doing?" Paisley hissed.

"It's called, 'being social.'" Ellie opened her menu, scanning the offerings. "Think of it as talking to people as if you are interested in their lives, not just what they know about a murder."

Paisley blanched at the definition but copied her friend. She smiled at the nearby couple before burying her nose in a list of dinner specials. "I thought you weren't ordering from the menu."

"I can dream."

The older couple responded to the girls' efforts. The husband leaned closer. "It's such a shock. Are you girls all right?"

"We're fine, thanks," Paisley said. "I'm sorry this has ruined your vacation."

"Ruined? Oh, no!" He scooted his chair closer. "Nothing this interesting ever happens when we go to Acapulco."

His wife cupped her hand to her mouth. "We heard the Newtons were swingers."

"Sweetheart," her husband admonished, "you have no idea what a swinger is. Besides, I believe adultery would be the more appropriate term. The wife is the main suspect, after all. That's what I gathered from the questions the police asked us. It's always the wife." He shot his wife a guilty look. "Present company excluded, Snookums."

"Not funny, Honey Bear," his wife wagged a finger at him. "Although, I did enjoy being interrogated. Have you seen that gorgeous U.S. Marshal that's running the investigation?"

Honey Bear briefly stuck out his tongue. "He's a bit full of himself."

"Kind of adorable, though, don't you think?" Snookums had a dreamy look on her face.

"Well, Agent Cruz certainly appeals to some women," Ellie laughed, and Paisley kicked her under the table.

"Do you know Mrs. Newton?" Paisley asked.

The husband lowered his voice. "I told the police about an old rumor. It's said the Newtons come to Bluebird for a 'cheating' vacation."

Paisley nodded, keeping Marika's revelation about Newton's love life to herself, and she was glad Ellie did, too. Although, her friend chugged half of the water in her glass and raised a finger at the waiter to bring more.

"He came to play, if you know what I mean." Honey Bear slanted a look at his ball and chain. "I've always doubted it was a joint venture. Who could get their wife to agree?"

"Not me, Honey Bear."

He went back to his cocktail, as the chef came over to their table.

Ellie looked up, surprised, admiring the French-born adonis. Chef Armand was on his way to being a celebrity. Chiseled, charming and creative in the kitchen, he wouldn't be cooking at the resort level for long. He greeted the ladies with open arms, a pro at interacting with his guests. "Ma cherie," he said, sprinkling his words with a few French ones. He took Ellie's hand. "I have created a masterpiece for you. Everything you have ever wanted in a meal. Shall we start with sirloin?"

Ellie's eyes lit up. "I love steak."

"Shouldn't we feed her fish?" Paisley asked, wanting to deep six the high cholesterol meal; along with Chef Armand's need to seduce a woman half his age. Well, not half his age. She had to admit, he was pretty much right between Ellie's age and her own.

"I have found the freshest of mushrooms, radishes and garbanzo beans to create your steak. It's meat-like consistency looks and tastes every bit as good as a sizzling sirloin. You will swear it came to you right off a Texas grill."

Ellie scrunched up her nose. It didn't sound as appetizing to her. "Okay, but what else? Baked potato with all the fixings?"

"No," Chef Armand waved off the idea like it was too common for his kitchen. "Saffron Rice!"

Paisley raised a finger. "Wouldn't wild rice or brown jasmine be healthier?"

"Healthy? Ah, mademoiselle, it is not any Saffron Rice. I take a head of cauliflower and chop it up so fine it looks like rice. Add saffron, cayenne, lime and cilantro...voila...a treat for your luscious mouth."

Ellie could only make a face. "So, it's not really steak and it's not rice."

He kissed her hand and backed away toward the kitchen. "I shall not disappoint."

"Thank you?" Ellie's stomach grumbled in agony. She mouthed the word 'help' to Paisley.

Without a second thought, Paisley hurried after the chef. He disappeared into the kitchen before she could get his attention, but she didn't let that stop her. Pushing through double doors, Paisley entered a kitchen full of activity.

Four sous chefs worked in unison around a central counter, plating food and getting it to waiters as fast as possible. The closest assistant spotted her and snapped his fingers. The sound alerted Chef Armand. He pivoted on his heel and held up his hand like a stop sign. "Oh, no, no, no. Distractions are not allowed, even in the form of a beguiling lady."

'He just can't stop himself,' Paisley realized, liking the compliment more than she cared to admit. "Excuse my intrusion, but I just wanted to say how much I appreciate you taking care of Ellie and her dietary needs," Paisley said, stepping out of the way of a waiter with a huge tray of food. "Can we just find a way to add something simple, yet delicious, to the menu? You might not have noticed, because Ellie is too sweet to let on, but she's having trouble with the new diet. We might lose her if we get too creative."

Chef Armand leaned against the counter, mindlessly picking up a sliver of carrot and munching on it. "I should have noticed. It is I who begs apology. I am losing my mind! It's the crazy police all over the place!" His raised voice caused the kitchen help to move a little quicker. "No, no, it's not you." He waved for them to slow down.

"Why would the police question you?" Paisley asked, her curiosity piqued.

"I am somewhat of a gastric genius," he said, bragging a little. "I cook with many unusual tools, like a cattle prod. And since it is missing, the police think I killed the awful Mr. Newton."

The revelation gave Paisley goosebumps. "So, I was right. Mr. Newton was killed by an electrical shock and they think it was from your cattle prod?"

"Why would I kill such a man?" he shrugged it off, but worry lined his brow.

"A cattle prod can't be strong enough to kill a man."

Chef Armand hated to admit it, but his cattle prod packed a bigger punch. "Most are relatively harmless powered by 9 volts. I use mine on Cowboy Night. As each steak comes off the grill... zzzap! It's for show, but we wanted a spark when it touched the meat."

"We?" Paisley asked, trying to think of some way to clear the chef of murder.

"Felicity Lange," he said, claiming themed dinner nights were her idea. "She had one of the resort's handy men up the voltage."

Paisley looked around the kitchen. "You said it's missing? Where do you keep it?"

Chef waved to an empty hook on the wall. "With the knives and other tools."

"Anyone could have taken it," Paisley said, knowing the fact helped the chef's situation. "Don't worry. It's pretty obvious that you didn't have a motive to kill Mr. Newton. Plus, anyone could have taken the cattle prod. I know the U.S. Marshal handling the investigation. He's good at his job and a fair man."

"Can I quote you on that?" Ellie interrupted, peeking through the kitchen's double doors.

Chef Armand instantly went to greet her. "Ma cherie! I must feed you."

"It's okay," Ellie sighed. "Less food is good for my figure."

He glanced at her hips. "We must never alter with perfection."

Ellie blushed, no longer caring about dinner. She could survive on his delicious compliments alone. A sudden burst of voices, however, interrupted her bliss. They echoed from the dining room, followed by a shriek!

The entrance of Mrs. Newton commanded everyone's attention. Hair a mess, makeup spotty, face puffy... she should have taken dinner in her room. Unfortunately, the new widow was on a mission. She made a slow pivot, scanning the dining room with pain-filled eyes.

"Where is she? Where is the hussy? Where is the fitness trainer that killed my husband?!" Even her pleasing Aussie accent couldn't turn Mrs. Newton's shrill screech into anything but an accusation.

At the kitchen's double doors, Paisley took a step back. All eyes shifted her direction.

Mrs. Newton zeroed in on her, panting like a wild animal. She pointed at Paisley. "A tryst wasn't enough? You had to torture him to death in your class?"

As a fitness trainer trying to jumpstart a career, Paisley's worst nightmare came true. The damage to her reputation could never be repaired! She didn't even know how to defend herself against a grieving widow, especially when she knew hateful gossip had to be the source. 'Brava, Vicki,' Paisley thought. 'You knew exactly where to do the most damage.'

"That is not true!" Ellie stepped forward. "Paisley did nothing to your husband. I'm sorry for your loss, but you don't know what you're saying."

Mrs. Newton balled up a fist, striking it at the air. An outburst welled up within, but the grieving widow's emotions were too out of control. Red splotches dotted her skin. She cried out like a cornered, wounded animal. She looked around for a 'weapon.' Settling on the closest thing—a bread basket—she grabbed a dinner roll and hurled it at Ellie's head.

The girl ducked out of the way. "Hey! I'm gluten-free now. Don't throw that stuff at me."

A second commotion erupted, as Dolan and Trooper Agnew rushed into the dining room. A waiter stepped aside to let them through. "Mrs. Newton," Dolan said, using a voice he normally reserved for his senile aunt or very young children, "we don't know who killed your husband, but he didn't die of natural causes."

"I know," she screeched. "Exercising killed him!" She took another bread roll from the basket and chucked it in Paisley's direction. It fell a bit short.

Dolan stepped in front of Mrs. Newton. "Ma'am, your husband didn't die because of a workout. He was electrocuted."

A gasp and nervous chatter filtered throughout the room.

"What?" Mrs. Newton looked confused. She really wanted to throw another roll, but all the fire in her deflated. "I don't understand. Someone really killed my Fig Newton?"

Dolan nodded for Agnew to lead her away. "The show's over, folks, please enjoy your meal." He gave the room a little wave, letting his eyes slant toward Paisley, before he followed Mrs. Newton and Agnew.

"Wow," Ellie said. "Now everyone knows you didn't kill Newton."

Wow, indeed, Paisley thought, mind reeling from the near disaster. She shook it off. "Sounds like Dolan might have a few solid leads."

"Oooh," Ellie laughed, heading back to their table. "Guess you might not solve the case before him. I hope you can live with that."

Paisley had no intention of conceding, in spite of Dolan clearing her name.

Chef Armand interrupted any more discussion with his gluten-free creations. With a flourish, he ushered a waiter forward. The man held a tray loaded with steaming masterpieces. Placing each dish in the middle of the table, Armand watched for Ellie's reaction. "Sample everything first, then see what you like best." He held his breath in anticipation of her first bite.

Eager to please, Ellie took a spoonful of the dish that looked like yellow rice. One taste made her toes curl. "It's so good!" She quickly tested every dish on the table, double-dipping into the fake steak. Her ooh's and aah's became moans of delight. "Food that's good for you can actually taste good!"

"My work is done." Chef Armand bowed his head before hurrying back to the kitchen.

Paisley couldn't have been more pleased by Chef Armand's success, but she was preoccupied with the few clues that separated her investigation from Dolan's official one. She believed her clues were unique and nothing he would ever consider. 'Should I tell him about my theories?' Paisley wondered. She decided not to bother Dolan until she found more compelling evidence. After all, she had more gut feelings than concrete facts, like how Mrs. Newton was wearing the same stinky perfume as Marika and the workout woman. 'I'd sound crazy to Dolan, since all I've got is an abundance of weird smelling perfume and silver bracelets.'

"I can't decide. Is it worse when you go on and on about solving Mr. Newton's murder, or when you keep quiet and just make faces?" Ellie asked, loading her plate with more of the gluten-free food.

"I'm making faces?"

"Maybe it's just how you think, but it looks very painful." Ellie savored every bite on her plate. "I love it here. I think I have to kidnap Chef Armand."

"He probably won't mind," Paisley said, absently, playing with her fork. She speared a grilled piece of broccoli. "What was all that really about with Mrs. Newton? Even if she heard Vicki's gossip, she had a tone."

"The I-need-a-valium tone?"

"Grieving, yes, but a little like a jealous wife." Paisley couldn't understand why. "Didn't she sound like a woman confronting a mistress?"

"Ew." Ellie shook her head. "Not while I'm eating, please."

Paisley wanted to believe the emotional outburst was grief, however the woman seemed bent on exposing something scandalous. It made Paisley wonder. "How many of Mr. Newton's mistresses do you think are staying at the resort right now? Maybe she thinks I'm one of them."

Ellie changed the subject. "You should really try the rice. I'm officially in love with cauliflower."

Shaking her head, Paisley felt certain she was right, and maybe it would help her solve the murder. "To catch the killer, maybe I should let everyone think I was having an affair with Mr. Newton!"

Chapter 5

No Time to Scream

The morning hiking group gathered in the lobby. It contained the usual suspects... the friendly couple from dinner, Snookums and Honey Bear, several die-hards with hiking sticks and familiar faces from Paisley's classes. One in particular stood out.

"That's her," Paisley hissed, letting her chin point the way.

From a corner near the lobby entrance, Paisley and Ellie watched the movements of the stylish workout lady who smelled like flowery urine perfume. She wore a purple tracksuit. They didn't have the correct angle to see a logo, but it looked expensive.

"Maybe you didn't see what you thought you saw during Mr. Newton's meltdown in your spin class," Ellie said. "The nice lady could have just been looking at you in sympathy."

"I don't think she was looking at me."

"Isn't she too classy to have an affair with Mr. Newton?" Ellie puckered her lips, unable to make the connection in her mind.

"How about me?" Paisley asked. She raised her wrist, showing off Mr. Newton's signature love token—a silver chain bracelet with a heart charm.

Ellie groaned. "I do not approve of this plan."

Paisley had bored Ellie with all her theories, and meaningless clues, late into the night. It seemed better to wait out the scandal, and let Dolan get to the truth. At least, Ellie suggested something along those lines. Paisley would have none of it.

"I'm doing this." Paisley pushed up her sleeves, so the bracelet was more noticeable. "I want to see who takes the bait and asks me about the affair."

Ellie cringed. "You really want people to think you had an affair with Mr. Newton? I thought we were trying to protect your job."

Shrugging off a possible complication, Paisley knew she'd be able to clear her good name on all counts, after she exposed the killer. Even if it meant maligning her virtue. "Technically, it would have been almost impossible for me to have any kind of liaison with Mr. Newton. His stay and our arrival only overlapped a day."

"Doesn't take long for one romantic encounter," Ellie cautioned, seeming to hint that it was very possible.

Paisley waved off the fact. "Besides, you're my witness that it never happened, and it's just a story to catch the killer."

"Lucky me," Ellie said, raising jazz hands to wave on either side of her face. "Do we really have to go on a treasure hunt to see who else is wearing a silver heart bracelet?"

"We have several treasure hunts today," Paisley said, cryptic as to what they were. "Let's start with the lady that loves her pink and purple. You know, when I was watching Newton through the window, complaining to Felicity, so was our mysterious lady."

"Okay, I'm helping. I'm here, right? I might as well aid and abet, since I can't talk any sense into you." However, Ellie was still a little fuzzy on her friend's plan. If it involved hiking, she was out. "I'm beginning to think my nose and pine trees don't get along." She sniffed to make her point.

"I've got a different kind of pine for you."

Squinting, Ellie couldn't think of any pine scent that would benefit their unofficial investigation.

"While we're out hiking, you are going to get into our mystery lady's room and snoop around." Paisley's eyes lit up, seeing nothing wrong with the suggestion.

Ellie couldn't speak for a moment, her mouth stuck between screaming and making a very rude noise.

"Maybe you can find something to connect her and Newton," Paisley reasoned, "like a silver bracelet with a heart charm. Although, a framed photograph of them together would be wonderful."

"I break into her room?" Ellie stepped to the side so Paisley's body blocked her view of the blonde in question. "I thought you'd be pressuring me to go on this stupid hike and make friends with her or something. I'm very good with people, and I need more exercise. Besides, the pine allergy thing was just an excuse."

"Good, because I'm pretty sure the maid service uses a pine cleaning solution in the bathrooms."

"You want me to be a maid?" Ellie slapped a hand over her mouth, containing her outburst.

Paisley looked over her shoulder, scanning the lobby. No one was paying any attention to them. "You'll only be pretending to be a maid. You'll mostly be sneaking into someone's room, which could be considered very athletic." Paisley made a face, finally getting it. "You're right. What am I asking you to do?"

While it would serve her right to let Paisley wallow in her misguided plan, Ellie actually considered doing it. "It is kinda like a secret mission, and I don't think it's illegal to impersonate a maid."

"Forget it," Paisley chided herself. "I was wrong. You can't break into her room."

"What if I temporarily worked for the resort? I wouldn't be pretending. I'll be employed. That's a loophole." Ellie had a plan of her own. "I only see one problem."

Paisley had to take a deep breath. "Cleaning toilets?"

"We don't seem to know mystery woman's name. How do I find her room?" Ellie squinted, happy to see something spark in her friend's eyes.

"Follow me." Paisley took off toward the mystery woman.

"I'll take that as you saying: 'Thanks Ellie. You're brilliant, Ellie. Couldn't do this without you, Ellie.' And praise like that." Ellie followed her toward a group waiting for the hike.

"Hello everyone," Paisley addressed the hikers. "We'll be leaving shortly for our hike. Please get ready to go. Now's a great time for a pitstop, unless you want to really commune with nature."

She got a laugh, mingling through the crowd, greeting a couple of the guests. She came up to the lady in purple last. "Weren't you in my spin class? It's nice to see you back. I'm sorry, I've been a little slow putting names to faces."

"Rachel Stenfield," the blonde filled in the blanks.

Having gotten the name she needed, Ellie pivoted in the other direction, almost colliding with the resort manager. "Oops! Sorry." Ellie scooted around her, making for the check-in desk.

"I hope you don't mind," Felicity ignored the near collision and spoke to Paisley. "I'll be joining you this morning. I need the fresh air."

Paisley tried to hide a groan, hoping the manager wasn't coming along to find a reason to fire her. But Felicity waved at the guests, acting like any other participant ready for a little exercise.

"See?" Felicity asked, super chipper.

The single-word question meant nothing to Paisley. "See what?"

"You didn't have to worry about your reputation. The guests love you and your classes. No one is connecting your training with poor Mr. Newton's passing." Felicity indicated the hiking group.

Paisley nodded, smart enough to understand what Felicity was really saying with her compliments.

"It would be a shame if you did something to change that." Felicity covered her manager's warning with a rare smile. It vanished just as quickly, however, when she noticed Paisley's bracelet. "Where did you get that?"

The sharp tone caught the attention of the head bellman, known as Mr. Gossip. His greedy eyes spotted the bracelet, too. He instantly sent out a group text: "Mistress #21 is so fit, she's fine. What was she thinking?"

He hurried back to work, none the wiser... except every employee on the text message, which was everyone but Paisley and Felicity.

Instantly regretting her plan, Paisley choked on her words, before getting out, "The gift shop. I bought the bracelet at the gift shop." It was the truth.

Felicity recovered her composure quickly. "You know, I heard you're taking us on the lake view hiking path. It's one of my favorites. I'm so glad you picked it."

With a nod to a couple of guests, Felicity moved ahead to do what she did best—take control. Nothing seemed to happen at the Bluebird without the manager's knowledge or approval. Paisley couldn't help but wonder what the woman knew about Mr. Newton's liaisons.

'If only I had the guts to ask,' Paisley thought. Of course, that would probably turn her warning into a written reprimand. She still had a strong suspicion that the resort manager was checking her out, looking for a reason to let her go. "Does everyone have a water bottle, sunscreen and good walking shoes?" she asked the crowd.

A hearty "yes" rose up from the group.

"Let's move outside where we'll begin with some dynamic stretches to wake-up our muscles, and we'll save the real stretching for after our hike to speed muscle recovery and re-balance our bodies."

Not everyone understood Paisley's instructions. A few talked among themselves about how there was more to hiking than they thought. As they filtered out the front entrance, one guest asked: "Will I burn enough calories to eat Chef Armand's banana creme pie?"

"Definitely," Paisley answered.

"I want pie, too, so I hope you have room for one more!" Dolan joined the group, wearing a well-used jogging outfit. "Hello, Felicity." He singled out the resort manager, giving Paisley the odd sensation that he considered her a suspect.

'He considers everyone a suspect,' Paisley remembered, silently keeping the fact to herself. "Well, how about that? We have our own private U.S. Marshal as an escort. Aren't we fancy and very safe. Everyone, let's head out the front door and take a left."

Felicity joined Snookums and Honey Bear, leading the way. Paisley hung back. She fell into step with Dolan. "What are you doing?"

"My job," he said, all business. "What are you doing?"

Paisley didn't know what he meant. "I'm leading a hike."

"Uh-huh!" his chin bobbed up and down. "And it's full of so many suspects. How'd you manage that?"

Looking at the back of most of the hiker's heads, Paisley tried to recall their faces. "Which ones are suspects?"

"That's my job," Dolan said. "Stick to yours."

They followed the group out. The crisp morning air made for a cool slap in the face. Perfect for their walk.

Rachel came up behind Paisley, as she picked up a backpack she'd left at the door. "I hope you give us a good workout. I need something to clear the cobwebs," Rachel said, looking fresh and amazing in spite of her words. Tiny diamond studs sparkled from her earlobes.

"I hope so," Paisley answered, squinting at the earrings and taking a sniff of the air near Rachel's shoulder. "Just smell that morning air."

"Hmm," Rachel mumbled moving ahead of her with a quick look back. "Yes, I love the pine smell."

Unfortunately, that's all Paisley smelled, too. She pouted, wondering why Rachel would wear perfume at spin class but not for the hike. "Duh!" she puffed out an exasperated breath of air, thinking, 'Rachel doesn't have to wear the perfume anymore. She doesn't have a rendezvous with Newton today.'

With a shot of adrenalin spurring her on, Paisley hurried to get to the front of the group. She had every hope of solving Newton's murder by the end of the day.

Five floors above the lobby and all the way at the back of the resort, Ellie stepped off the service elevator dressed like a Grand

Teton Bluebird Resort maid with a name tag claiming her as Anna.

"This way, Anna," a real maid said, pushing a cart full of cleaning supplies and toiletries to restock guest bathrooms. In the center, a big bin waited for the dirty linens. The maid pointed to the first room. "Make it as clean as you can, as fast as you can."

Ellie pulled a face. Suddenly, she didn't particularly like undercover work.

After cleaning two rooms, Ellie longed to sink into her own bed for a nap; however, she earned praise from her new cleaning mentor for filling in when several of the staff quit. They had been spooked by the death.

"Only three-hundred and forty-seven rooms left," the maid said, pointing Ellie to her next one. Weary eyes brightened when she saw the room number.

Entering Rachel Stenfield's one-bedroom suite, Ellie instantly went into the bathroom. She peeked into a makeup bag without touching anything. Her hope was to see the bracelet, but it was stuffed of makeup. The only thing that seemed out of place was a full bottle of Linger perfume in the trash. She loved the scent, and slipped it into one of the big pockets in her uniform. She set the rest of the trash by the door for dumping.

Poking her head out the door, she could hear the other maid humming to herself somewhere in the next suite. She still had time to snoop. Racing back into the bedroom, she opened drawers and peeked into the closet. A tiny safe caught her attention. It was cracked open just enough to see inside. She couldn't be sure what kind of treasure it held, but it looked like something was inside.

Ellie stuck her head into the closet to get a better look.

"What are you doing?" the maid's voice snapped from the hallway door.

Ellie gasped. She stepped out of the closet, thinking quickly and grabbed an iron off the closet shelf. "Aren't we supposed to put this stuff away?"

The maid nodded, laughing off her mistake. "I got this," she said, picking up the trash bin by the door. "Make the bed."

Ellie turned to the king sized bed and its messy, tangled sheets. Her lip curled into a snarl.

The hiking path took them upward through majestic sequoias and along a mountain creek. Its gurgling melody tripped over rocks and boulders on it's way to the lake.

Paisley kept the group together, pointing out birds and reminding them to engage their core and watch their step. "Oh, look, a bluebird." She pointed at a nearby tree. The hikers stopped and quickly captured the bird on their cell phone cameras.

Reaching the top of their climb, the group stopped for a well-earned break. Paisley passed out water bottles and energy bars. "A snack is very important for hikes. You need to maintain your blood sugar levels."

"Do tell," Dolan encouraged, even if it sounded like teasing.

"A snack of 100 to 200 calories is perfect," Paisley finished her mini lecture.

Dolan stretched his arms wide, appearing to need no snack or rest. He followed Paisley around, as she handed out the treats. He even helped a lady open her water bottle cap. "I can never open the sports bottle kind," she sighed.

"Happy to be of use," Dolan's charm had the lady smiling over her deficiency.

When they'd almost emptied Paisley backpack, Dolan stepped forward for his treats. "Don't forget me."

"How could I?" Paisley asked. "Do I get an update on your investigation?"

"Why would you need that?" he asked "You're leaving it to the authorities."

Paisley handed him the last snack bar and water bottle. "I'm on your side, sir. When are you going to realize that?"

He took a moment to let her squirm. "The preliminary coroner's report supports your electrocution theory," Dolan said, revealing nothing new. "What angle are you working on?"

Paisley paused, waiting for a couple of guests to pass by. She pointed to the vista. "This is a great spot for a selfie, but be careful of the edge."

The rough path twisted near the cliff overlooking the lake and meandered back into a dense collection of trees. Several guests dared to get close to the cliff for the best shot.

"No angle, but I would never consider Chef Armand as a suspect." She took a sip from her water bottle.

"Who says we have?"

"Chef Armand," Paisley smiled, knowing he didn't need to worry. "His missing cattle prod could have been the murder weapon."

Dolan disagreed. "Cattle prods aren't strong enough to kill cows or humans."

"Unless..." Paisley hummed a little fanfare tune, "the cattle prod has been juiced up enough to cook meat."

Dolan chewed on that a minute, grumbling, "You know this for a fact, don't you?"

"It came up in conversation," Paisley explained.

Interrupting, Dolan barked, "Stop interviewing my witnesses!"

A few of the guests looked their way. "Wouldn't it be easier to thank me?" Paisley asked.

Dolan huffed, breathing heavily through his nostrils. He stared at the view. The glorious vista did not improve his mood. The postcard perfect panorama took in the resort's lodge, lake, boardwalk and dock.

Paisley noticed most of the houseboats were moored. It made her remember something. "Did you know that the resort named a boat after Mr. Newton?"

He brushed the information aside. "I know you think this is a game, but it's not. A killer walks among us. Unless, it was some crazy random act, which is unlikely due to the personal nature of the attack, anyone around us could be the killer. None of the guests have mysteriously fled. All the people that were here when Newton died are still here. Let that sink in a minute the next time you go and play detective."

She stared at the ground, hating every minute they spent arguing.

Dolan filled the empty space between them, reaching for her arm. "I'm sorry, I just don't want to encourage you. Really, we got this. You can stand down, now. Your reputation is in the clear. We've got a couple of really good leads that I'm confident will pan out soon."

"What leads?" Paisley asked sweetly.

He had no intention of pulling her further into the investigation.

Paisley made a sound that could be interpreted as a congratulatory grunt, however it was more like she'd embraced a challenge. She held firm. If anyone was going to solve Mr. Newton's murder, it had to be her. If Dolan expected her to give up, he'd need to try harder to solve the mystery first.

She glanced around, checking on the other hikers. They looked almost ready to go, tucking away their trash for the walk back and coming out from under the shade to explore their mountain perch. No one needed her.

Dolan brushed his hand against Paisley's. "You don't seem to get it. When I'm worried about a case, you should be petrified."

She only shook her head.

"So you're still going to investigate?" He bit on his tongue to stop himself from cussing.

"Why did you have to come up here?" Paisley's voice was barely above a whisper.

"Why did you uproot your life and take my sister with you?" Dolan had no intention of opening up, unless she did first.

Paisley leaned into his shoulder for the briefest moment. "If you're here to save me, and hoping it will save us, you need to know that it won't. I'm sorry, but I'll never be able to trust you with my heart again." It hurt to say the words aloud. Somehow, it made the end of their relationship real.

She could see that he wanted to say something, but he needed a minute.

"Ellie's here because she needs my help," Paisley continued, filling the awkward moment by answering the rest of his question. "She needs less judging and more support. Celiac disease is real. I can help her. I want to help her. She'll always be a sister of my heart."

Dolan nodded. Sad eyes lowered. "Okay... for now, but you're playing with fire... when it comes to this investigation." Doing his job was the easiest course to take. Dolan squared his shoulders, instantly becoming the no-nonsense lawman. He stepped away, and started up a conversation with Snookums and Honey Bear.

Paisley had a sinking feeling that she should have waited until after the investigation to tell Dolan that he didn't have a chance to make things right. 'You stupid girl,' she silently chided herself.

A man with a walking stick waved for assistance, requiring Paisley to hurry over. "Is everything all right?"

"Can you take my picture?" he asked, rather loudly.

It also caused Felicity and Rachel to come to his aid. The three women collided, as the man's camera fell to the ground.

"Oh!" Paisley uttered, feeling the ground shift under her feet. Gravity took control, as her right foot slid toward the cliff and her

world suddenly tipped sideways toward a
hundred and fifty foot drop!

Chapter 6

All's Well that Ends Well

A strong hand caught Paisley's wrist, mid-air, as her feet lost the battle with gravity. In one strong yank, she was back on solid ground in Dolan's arms. She breathlessly mumbled a thanks, unable to stop shaking. For a moment she let him hold her close. He felt like home, but then she remembered... and pulled away.

"Oh, my gosh!" The rosy color drained from Rachel's cheeks. "Are you okay? I'm so sorry."

"Move back," Felicity ordered, "unless you want to push her off the cliff again."

Rachel retreated, eyes downcast.

The other hikers rushed to their aid.

"Thank goodness you were close enough to save her," Honey Bear said, keeping a tight hold on his wife's hand.

Paisley decided to downplay the near disaster. She knew how close she came to falling and wondered if Rachel really pushed her, but now wasn't the time to cause a panic. Reading Felicity's nervous energy, she knew how this would look for the resort. Paisley needed to do something so the group wouldn't spread more rumors of how deadly the resort was for visitors.

"It's my fault," Paisley blurted, taking a step away from Dolan. "Thank you all for your quick reactions. I certainly demonstrated how not to ignore your surroundings. Hiking is safe, but nature doesn't come with a safety net... unless you bring along a well-trained U.S. Marshal."

The attention shifted to Dolan. He took the praise with a little squint at Paisley. He might not have understood what she was doing, but Felicity did. She took Paisley by the arm and lead her away from the group.

"Did she push you?" Felicity kept her voice low so they wouldn't be overheard.

Paisley tried to smooth over the whole thing. "It was an accident."

Felicity wasn't as sure. "I wouldn't admit this to the police, because it's gossip… but Rachel and Mr. Newton were more than friends."

"Are you saying he gave her a heart bracelet?" Paisley glanced at Felicity's wrists. She wasn't wearing any jewelry, today. "They were Mr. Newton's go-to gift."

"I should ask how you know that, and if you really bought your own bracelet. No matter. However—and this stays between us," Felicity demanded, "Rachel and Newton's trips to our resort frequently coincided. So much so, it couldn't have been an accident, more like a regular rendezvous."

"Why wouldn't you tell the police?" Paisley felt it was her duty.

"The authorities have all our records," Felicity explained. "All I have is gossip. I'm confident the facts will come out once they've assembled all the evidence."

Paisley had to admit that Rachel was now at the top of her suspect list.

"OMG! Are you all right? You look all right. I sure hope you're ready to give up this crazy investigation!" Ellie jogged up to her friend on the boardwalk, wearing stylish teal and grey workout clothes. She glistened from putting them to use, but it didn't stop her from giving Paisley a quick, sweaty hug.

"Look at you, actually jogging," Paisley said, taking in the outfit. "And, yes, I'm fine. And, no, I'm not giving up."

Groaning, Ellie unzipped her jacket to cool down. "Dolan texted me about your near-death experience and how I needed to be careful. He said you were fine, but I couldn't take his word. I had to see for myself."

"It was an accident." Paisley glossed over the facts. She didn't want to worry her friend, and was sorry that Dolan got to her first. She had been delayed by the hikers. "I'm surprised to find you out here. Aren't you exhausted from your new job?"

"I had to clean out my nasal passages from all the cleaning chemicals. That stuff they use to disinfect everything—and I mean everything—it can't be healthy to breathe. I would say something to management," Ellie admitted, "if we didn't need to keep my little side job on the down low."

"What did you learn?"

Ellie bent one foot up, grabbing it with a hand. The calf stretch made her unsteady. She had to release it. "How do people jog every day? I'm already sore."

"What did you learn?" Paisley coaxed.

"Well... I really respect maids."

The revelation wasn't quite what Paisley had hoped to hear. "Anything else?"

"Oh, yeah," Ellie had the biggest smile, "Rachel has a whole stack of files in her bedroom safe."

"Files?"

"Those thick brown kind. You know." Ellie rolled the image around in her mind. "I've seen those kind of files before. Can't remember where."

Paisley latched onto the clue. "Did you look at them? Take pictures of the content? Tell me... what did you do?"

"I made her bed." Ellie was proud of herself.

"About the files! What was in them?" Paisley bit her lip. "Did you take one?

Ellie threw up her hands. "What could I do? The rooms don't clean themselves. Plus, I had a supervisor. I was only there to observe, not steal. However, I did take a bottle of perfume, because she'd thrown it away. Get this, Rachel tossed a full bottle of Linger cologne."

"You took her perfume?"

"It was in the trash," Ellie pouted. "It's expensive stuff, and I used up the tiny bottle I had. It went fast and I only used it for special events."

Paisley knew that scent. "Is that the one you wore to our engagement party?"

Ellie didn't want to confirm or deny. She had a feeling it would backfire.

"That's the stuff Rachel was wearing during my spin class."

The insult did not miss Ellie. "You mean the one you said smelled like flowery urine? You think it smelled like that when I wore it?"

"It's probably just my nose," Paisley said, quickly changing the subject. "Marika was wearing it, too. I wonder if that means anything?"

Ellie frowned. "More women with bad taste in perfume?"

"You have to help me sniff it out. If you smell that scent on anyone else, let me know." Paisley already knew one way to connect Rachel and Marika—the late Mr. Newton. 'And now the perfume,' Paisley thought, but she wasn't sure if it was a good motive for murder.

"We're talking about perfume. It's supposed to make you smell good, not like a bathroom at a frat house." Ellie couldn't wrap her head around how anyone could think Linger perfume smelled bad. Especially since it was a fragrance she loved.

"I think you have time to make another lap," Paisley said, checking her watch.

"And what are you going to do?" Ellie zipped up her workout jacket.

"I'm going to check out the boats." Paisley skirted the question with an answer she hoped sounded like she wanted to rent one.

Although, she really just wanted to find the one named after Mr. Newton.

Ellie sighed. "Guess if you fall this time, you'll only get wet." She saw right through her, and knew persuading her friend to drop the investigation would be useless. With a little wave, she headed along the boardwalk for another trip around the lake.

Paisley turned onto the boat dock, as the sun dipped toward the mountain tops, beginning its downward descent. She'd have just enough time to inspect the boats before her next class. With a little notepad, she wrote down each boat's name as she passed its spot on the dock.

Several boat slips were empty, and she realized they were out on the lake. Luckily, their names were carved into little signs at each mooring slip. 'They do love their signs at the Grand Teton Bluebird Resort,' Paisley thought. 'Someone has an over-organized mind.' She couldn't help but think of the resort manager. Felicity! With a sigh, Paisley wondered how much the efficient woman knew about her guests, and if she could be pumped for more information about Mr. Newton.

"Don't do it!"

'Agnew?' Paisley thought, turning to find the handsome trooper taking in the stunning lake view.

"Local myth claims we have a monster in the lake," he said, joining her on the dock. "So, don't go out there unless you can swim."

"I haven't heard that one," Paisley had to admit. "Should I picture the Creature from the Black Lagoon or something fishier?"

One eyebrow rose. "You joke, but our little version of the Lochness Monster is called the Teton Tease. He likes to tip over boats."

"What a useful excuse for beginning boaters," Paisley said, slipping her notebook into a jacket pocket. She couldn't help but notice that Agnew's eyes followed the motion.

Paisley wasn't so sure anything could tip over the Bluebird's boats. They were ten-foot in length and built on pontoons. It would take a lot to turn them over and she'd never even seen a wave on the lake.

As if he could read her mind, Agnew nodded toward the water. "I know it's hard to believe on a day like today." The lake was crystal clear and smooth as glass. "When the wind picks up, you don't want to be out there."

"You know everything about this place, don't you?" Paisley hoped knowing a true local would help her investigation.

"It's home," he said. "I'd do anything to protect it."

"I'll remember," Paisley said. "Were you looking for me?"

"I'm surprised to find you here," he said, letting his eyes linger on her jacket pocket. "You've been cleared of all wrong doing. Aren't you teaching again?"

"My late afternoon spin class is full, but I could find room for you." Paisley couldn't help but offer. Something about the trooper intrigued her. 'Pride,' she decided. 'He lives and breathes this place. It must have been hard to give up the investigating to Dolan.'

"I never finished questioning you, and although your boyfriend—"

"Don't call him that," Paisley blurted. She had to interrupt. "Please."

He held up his hands. "My mistake."

Taking a deep breath, Paisley realized she'd overreacted. She'd also been over analyzing the trooper, which didn't help. "I'm sorry. I didn't mean to snap. I suppose I'm not the only one that wasn't happy to see Agent Cruz arrive to save the day."

Agnew had the good sense to only smile. He wasn't about to vent publicly. "I'm glad he was here to save you. What really happened on the hike?"

"Is that one of the questions you needed to ask me?"

"Actually, I wanted to know how long you're staying in the area." Agnew made no move to take out his notepad. However, he studied her facial expressions as if he were looking for some kind of tell, or indication of her intentions.

"I was hired for three months," Paisley explained, "and Ms. Lange has assured me that I'll be staying for the full term. Why? Have you heard something?"

He finally took out his notepad, flipping it open and scanning his notes. "Not at all, but I'm beginning to think you're paranoid." He found a blank page, pen poised over it. "I'll need your phone number."

Paisley bit her lip. "For follow up questions?"

"Or advice," he said. "I've noticed that you are very interested in this case."

She couldn't tell if he really wanted her help or if he was flirting. Any assumption could get her into trouble. "I had an interest while my class was considered a cause of death."

"But now that you're cleared?" he asked, letting the question hang for her to fill in the blanks.

Paisley stepped closer, took his pen and wrote her cell phone number on the pad. When she handed the pen back, his hand engulfed hers. She looked up into his quizzical expression. It held more tenderness than she'd expect from someone who maintained a stern exterior. With her, however, he let down his guard.

"I have a curious mind and I'm glad to help," Paisley said, feeling the need to create some distance between them. The last thing she wanted to do was flirt with a man working with her ex-fiance, even if it was temporary.

"Is that why you're down here?" he asked, motioning to the boats.

She blinked, considering what she should say and what she should leave out. "I think one of these boats was named after Mr. Newton."

He walked further onto the boat dock. His eyes scanned the vessels. "Gooseberry, Indian Plum, Rusty Fig," he read off the boat names closest to him. "Sounds like a fruit theme to me."

"You're right," Paisley had to agree. "I expected one to be named after a very popular cookie."

"Fig Newton," they both said at the same time.

"Do they use rusty figs to make Fig Newtons?" Agnew wondered.

Paisley shook her head, no. "Rusty figs are found in Australia."

Agnew cocked his head to the side, considering her with an amazed expression. "How did you know that?"

"I read a lot." Paisley turned to the Rusty Fig's boat slip. It was empty, but had they found the right boat? "Mr. Newton was Australian."

Agnew clapped a hand against his notepad. "Bravo, but what does it mean?"

"You've been looking for people that wanted to kill Mr. Newton," Paisley said, lumping him in with all the other agents and detectives on the case.

"The list keeps growing," Agnew admitted.

"What about people that liked him?" Thinking through her logic out loud felt good, especially since someone other than her closest friend was actually listening to her. She paced the width of the dock, working it out. "It's a shorter list. There's his wife."

"She has an alibi," Agnew added.

"There's anyone he tipped," she continued.

"We've almost ruled out the whole staff," Agnew said. "And as you've implied, they had more to lose than to gain from Newton's death. Plus, they are skilled at dealing with difficult guests."

'The Grand Teton Bluebird Resort definitely had its share of diva clients,' Paisley thought. She realized he was right. 'If the killer was someone on staff, they wouldn't have killed him due to resort business. It had to be personal.'

"I see the wheels turning," Agnew cocked his head to the side to see her face better. "What else?"

"Mr. Newton had affairs with the guests, with the staff... but that was normal for him."

"Was it normal for you?" Agnew asked, an eyebrow rising.

Paisley could tell the gossip she'd planted had reached him. She wasn't sure what to say, but quickly decided on the truth. "I wasn't here long enough to fall under Mr. Newton's spell, but I know several women did."

Paisley felt an unseen tug on her conscious. Her adrenalin kicked up a notch, her body tingled with the challenge. She loved solving puzzles, especially when she experienced a knowing sensation that she was on the right track. Her gut feeling told her to ignore distracting clues and follow the ones that rang true.

"I don't know," Agnew voiced a reoccurring theme spouted by most law enforcement. "You want us to investigate people that appeared to want him alive? It's not standard procedure."

"I want to know who named the boat after him." Paisley turned away, heading back to the boardwalk.

Agnew fell into step with her long stride. "Are you saying that the person who named the boat after Newton is the one that killed him?"

"I'd never say that," Paisley said with a smirk, "because I'm not investigating the murder."

"You're not?" he had to ask, but it sounded more like teasing.

"I'm just a girl with a curious mind." Paisley waved her hand, spotting Ellie finishing her lap around the lake. She pointed to the resort. Nearly spent, Ellie gladly veered off the boardwalk, onto the path up to the lodge.

"If you find any proof..." Agnew began.

"I'll let you know." Paisley winked, as she went to catch up with her friend.

Agnew closed his notepad, sucking in air as he watched her jog up the path to join Ellie. His lips parted and he whispered: "Be careful."

Chapter 7

Murder Multiplied

"Who cares who named the boat after Mr. Newton?" Ellie punched the number to their floor, impatiently waiting for the elevator doors to shut. "It's probably a handy man or something."

Paisley cared, but was too tired to explain.

"Hold the door!" a female voice shouted, high heels clacked their way to the elevator.

Paisley grabbed the door to keep it from shutting but almost let it go when she saw who she was helping. "Mrs. Newton!"

The widow looked a little more elegant and put together than yesterday. She stalled at the threshold, but finally entered and pushed the button for her floor. "I suppose you expect me to apologize." She faced the door but could see them in its reflective silver finish.

"Not necessary," Paisley assured her. "Everyone handles grief differently. You aren't yourself right now."

"It never ends!" she barked. "I'd leave this dreadful place, if the police would let me."

Ellie ho-hummed the widow's prickly attitude. "Awful being a murder suspect, isn't it?"

Mrs. Newton missed the comparison between her situation and how she'd accused Paisley. "I'm hardly a real suspect," she whined.

Ellie sniffed the air, leaning closer to the widow's teased-up hairdo. Paisley poked her in the arm to back off.

"I was minutes away from a divorce," Mrs. Newton spat out like it should mean as much to them as it did to her. "In fact, we were gathering some very damaging facts to clinch my case."

"We?" Paisley asked, mortified when Ellie sniffed the air again.

"Do you have a cold?" the older woman turned to look Ellie up and down. "Don't stand so close to me."

"You were getting a divorce," Paisley prompted, "so why would you murder your husband?"

"Exactly!" Mrs. Newton deemed her worthy enough to talk face to face. "I wanted all his dirty secrets to come out in court."

"Who wouldn't?" Paisley asked. "So, you have someone else here, working on compiling the case evidence with you?"

The elevator binged, stopping at Mrs. Newton's floor. "I hate talking about the divorce now. He was still the love of my life, the shit. I only wanted to destroy him in court, now I have to play the grieving widow when I'm only partly grieving." She dramatically stepped out of the elevator. The whole topic appeared to exhaust her.

Paisley made a face, finally smelling what Ellie noticed earlier. As the elevator door closed, she turned to her friend. "She wears Linger perfume!"

Ellie laughed. "Took you long enough. Does that mean you're getting used to the awful smell?"

Reaching their own floor, they headed down the long hallway. "I knew the perfume meant something. It's rather brilliant," Paisley said, figuring out why the cologne was important. "What's something that can accidentally expose an affair?"

"Not deleting your browser history?"

"Another woman's scent on your husband!" Paisley knew she was right. "Newton had all his ladies wear the same perfume as his wife, so he'd always smell like her, no matter who he was with! It's kinda brilliant."

"Or he could have taken a shower."

Paisley agreed but saw a catch. "It's pretty close quarters with them all being at the same resort. His hookups would need to be short. Might not always have time to clean up. How long could he really be away from his wife before she'd get suspicious? The length of a massage? A game of tennis?"

"Sounds like she was already suspicious." Ellie pointed out. "The divorce."

"We need to figure out who's been helping her get the dirt on Newton." Paisley was already running through a mental list of everyone she'd met at he resort. "It could be someone that knows everyone, like Felicity, or someone that also has a gripe with Newton."

Reaching their door, Ellie took out her key card. "Let's order room service."

"We just ate."

"I was thinking coffee on our little balcony." Ellie pulled out the key card and tried again. "I wish coffee tasted as good as it smells. Of course, that's why they make cream." Ellie jiggled the card. The little red light showed that the door was still locked. "My key is broken."

Paisley dug into her pocket. "Let's talk murder suspects. I think Mrs. Newton is off the list."

"Maybe more than just her," Ellie said, standing back so Paisley could get to the door. "I heard some hotel staff gossip, lots actually, but I had to ignore all the stuff about you and your bracelet. I found out that a lot of the suspects are going home soon. When their vacations end, the police don't have any evidence to make anyone stay. If you want to impress Dolan with your investigative skills, time's running out."

"That's not why I'm doing this." Paisley hated the assumption, opening the door on her first try. "Let's focus on the suspects. There's Rachel..."

"...who tried to push you off the cliff."

"Allegedly," Paisley said, bending to pick up a note that had been slipped under their door. "And there's Marika, the ex-lover, but maybe she still had a thing for Newton and couldn't take him buying all that jewelry for other women."

"She just snapped!" Ellie said, playing along but going to the room's landline.

"Hmm..." Paisley considered the theory, holding the unopened note. "Marika just didn't come across that way. She seemed like she still loved the guy."

"Go back to Rachel," Ellie said. "Why would she push you off the cliff? What have you done to her?"

Paisley thought it over for a minute. "She saw me with Newton at spin class and she could have heard the rumors we started. Jealousy?"

"After he died? Maybe she thinks you did it." Ellie shook off the idea, giving up for a moment to push a button on the hotel phone.

Paisley opened the note.

"What about the women we haven't discovered and their jealous husbands?" Ellie interrupted herself to speak into the phone. "Hello! Room service? We'd like coffee. A big, big pot of your most delicious coffee, and can you add extra cream and sugar? Thank you!" She hung up. "I should have ordered a gallon of Salted Caramel ice cream. I can't be expected to lose weight under these conditions."

"No!" Paisley shouted, going for her cell phone.

"I know," Ellie had to admit. "Salted caramel is so trendy. How about mint chocolate chip? I could call back."

Handing her friend the note, Paisley punched a contact on her cell phone. "Dolan? You have to find Rachel Stenfield right now. I think she's going to kill herself!"

The local troopers kept curious guests away from Rachel's room, including Paisley and Ellie. They waited in the wide hallway with a small group of curious onlookers. No one had a clue what had happened. Paisley considered using her connection with Dolan to get inside, but she waited until he came out and spotted them. His look told her all she needed to know.

Rachel was dead.

Walking the girls away from the crowd, Dolan took a deep breath. "How did you know?"

Paisley handed him the note. "I guess she slid it under our door."

"It's so weird," Ellie said, her voice low.

Dolan gave her a quick glance, concerned. She wrinkled her nose at him to stop, so he read the note, quickly calling for a trooper to bag it as evidence. "It looks like a suicide. She must have felt the walls closing in, although I have to admit, she wasn't a prime suspect by any means." He shook his head, as if admonishing himself.

"What about the files?" Paisley asked. "Did you find them in her closet?"

He let out a puff of exasperation. "What files?"

Paisley and Ellie shared a look. They hadn't planned on telling him like this, but it was too late for secrets. "She had a bunch of files in her room," Paisley admitted.

"What kind of files?" Dolan asked.

"I didn't actually see them," Paisley said, looking at Ellie.

"They were brown, full of paperwork and in her closet," Ellie said, bitting her lip and bracing herself for more questions—ones she didn't want to answer.

Dolan looked between them for a moment, clearly trying to decide what to ask next. "So, now, I'm looking for a bunch of files?"

"They could be important." Paisley knew she was pushing it with Dolan, but he seemed open to advice, although she doubted it would last.

"Should I ask how you saw the files?"

Paisley stuck her hands into her jean pockets. "No, no you should not."

He shook his head, seeming to chalk it up to chance not skill.

Paisley wanted to say something, as not to diminish their efforts; however, mentioning Ellie's foray into housekeeping could make things worse. She kept the fact to herself. "How much do you know about Mr. Newton's pending divorce? We had it straight from Mrs. Newton that she was ready to take him to court."

"She told me, too," Dolan said, making a little sound that hinted at his frustration. "Who haven't you interviewed?"

"We just ran into her in the elevator," Paisley explained.

"And you instantly became best buddies to the point she told you everything about her divorce case?" Dolan's voice rose as he spoke.

"That's it!" Ellie interrupted. "That's where I saw them!"

Proud of herself for remembering, Ellie waited for her brother to respond. When he didn't she turned to Paisley. "You know, I said I'd seen some like them somewhere."

Paisley took a deep breath, motioning for Ellie to follow her calming example. "Just slow down and tell us from the beginning—wait! You know where you saw them?"

Ellie nodded, as Paisley grabbed her friend's arms, excited.

Dolan had no clue. He raised a hand. "Could someone explain it to me?"

"Where did you see Rachel's folders before?" Paisley asked.

"Small claims court."

"Oh my gosh," Paisley gushed, "she must have been the one working with Mrs. Newton on the divorce!"

The girls high-fived.

Dolan still didn't understand completely, but he signaled another trooper. "Get Mrs. Newton down here. And where's Agnew? We need everyone." His attention went back to the girls, along with some disdain. "I knew you were investigating, but Paisley!" Dolan's face glowed red. "You put yourself in terrible danger. That hiking accident wasn't an accident at all. She tried to cover her tracks by getting rid of you."

"Maybe," Paisley shrugged "but I don't know how she knew during the hike. Ellie hadn't even gotten into her room yet."

Dolan leveled disapproving eyes at her, then his sister.

"We didn't break any laws," Ellie said. "I can show you my paycheck to prove it."

He did a double take at the mention of a paycheck, but knew that part of their story had to wait. "Where are the divorce files?" he sighed, running a hand through his hair. It left an enticing, messy tousle.

Paisley fought the impulse to reach out and mess it up even more. She liked him looking rough and ready, however it was a line she didn't want to cross. "Check Rachel's closet."

Dolan lead them back to Rachel's room, dispersing some of the crowd as he passed. "Get back to your rooms, please. Nothing to see here."

A trooper stopped Dolan as soon as they stepped inside. Paisley's eyes swept the room. It looked normal. All the activity was in the bathroom. "Not another bath tub death?" Paisley found it hard to believe.

Ellie hung back, afraid to see something she couldn't unsee.

Dolan went to the closet, opening the doors wide. A couple of dresses hung inside, but no files. He gave Paisley an exasperated look. She motioned at the safe. "She treated 'em like gold."

The safe was closed. Dolan had to summon Felicity to open it. She arrived quicker than expected and had the safe open in seconds. Unfortunately, it was empty inside and this time, Paisley was out of suggestions. She stepped back from all the police activity, finding herself shoulder to shoulder with the resort manager. They exchanged sad expressions. "What are you doing here?" Felicity asked with no reproof.

"Nothing useful, it would seem." Paisley headed for the door.

"You don't look happy," Ellie said, picking at a salad.

Paisley had no taste for her food, either. "Look at them." Her eyes raked the other diners, laughing and chatting as if nothing bad had happened.

It took most of the morning for the news of Rachel's demise and the end of Newton's murder case to make the rounds. In response, the guests had returned to normal resort life, filling the Grand Teton Bluebird Resort dining room with a party-like atmosphere. Not that conversations didn't touch on the murder mystery, but it also covered how to enjoy their day—on the lake or renting bikes. Life moved on, as the tragedy and fear faded into another curious bit of local history.

"I'm just happy to share a meal without discussing a murder," Ellie sighed, reaching for a breadstick and hiding a yawn. They'd rehashed every clue, aided by three pots of room service coffee, until the wee-hours of the morning. Ellie had crashed before her friend, but she'd hung in long enough to earn a medal. Even though Rachel's suicide didn't perfectly fit what they knew, she trusted her brother and the police to put everything right.

Paisley nodded like she was listening, even agreeing with Ellie's relief. Glancing around the room, however, she was far from pleased with what she saw. It's now or never, she thought. Squaring her shoulders, she spoke a bit louder than necessary, as if she wanted their conversation to be overheard. "I know there are copies of the divorce files and I'm going to find them!"

"What?" Ellie asked, instantly choking on a mouthful of lettuce. "Thh-There's nothing to find."

"I couldn't disagree more," Paisley continued in a voice meant to be heard throughout the lunch crowd. "The police have it all wrong. I think the missing Newton divorce files will prove the real killer is still at large!"

A hush fell over the dining room.

Ellie sunk a bit lower in her chair.

Paisley stood up, banging her fist firmly on the table. "I'm certain that Rachel wasn't Mr. Newton's killer!"

Gasps and nervous chatter circled the room.

"Wha-what?" Ellie stuttered.

"The files will prove it," Paisley declared. "And Rachel left me a clue about how to find her backup copies. I'm going to find them and expose the real killer!"

Ellie motioned for Paisley to sit or at least lower her voice. "Can you do that after lunch?"

"No, this is more important than lunch." Paisley stabbed the air with a finger. "I will find Mr. Newton's real killer!"

"She really needs eight hours of sleep," Ellie told the closest table.

"Excuse, me. I can't eat when I know the police have pinned Mr. Newton's murder on the wrong person!" Paisley dramatically headed out of the dining room. All eyes followed her, then slowly turned to Ellie.

"I don't have to eat, either. Although, lunch is a very important meal of the day." She grabbed a handful of breadsticks and ran after Paisley.

In the lobby, her friend was waiting near the front desk. Ellie threw up a hand, immediately demanding if Paisley had lost her freaking mind. "Are you forgetting that you already got what you wanted: restoring your good name and setting yourself up as a level-headed fitness instructor? If that little bit of theater gets back to Felicity—or Dolan—you could lose both!"

Paisley found it hard to contain her excitement. "I've got a plan."

"I'm pretty sure that I already hate it." Ellie nibbled on a couple of the breadsticks at the same time. "Your little rant is going to spread through this place like wildfire."

"That's what I'm hoping," Paisley said, motioning for Ellie to follow. "We need to make a show of going on some kind of treasure hunt throughout the resort."

It wasn't how Ellie had planned to spend her afternoon. "Chef Armand promised to give me a cooking lesson."

"Ellie Cruz," Paisley admonished, "you can flirt after we catch the killer."

Munching on more breadsticks, Ellie scrunched up her nose. "But there aren't any backup files to find."

"The killer doesn't know that." Paisley headed for the gift shop.

Following her, Ellie looked at the remaining breadstick. "I wish you were an ice cream cone."

Returning to their bedroom after an exhaustive show of searching for clues, a brusque, male voice greeted them.

"I've been waiting for over an hour!" Dolan sat in the room's one overstuffed chair, his dress shirt appeared a bit wrinkled after a long day.

"Oh!" Ellie exclaimed, taking a moment to recognize her brother. "What are you doing here?"

He got up from the chair and went to Paisley. "How'd it go?"

"Perfectly. You should have seen their faces." They bumped fists.

"You should see mine," Ellie snorted. "Are you in on this?"

Dolan leaned against the wall, as Ellie flopped on the bed. Paisley was too pumped up to sit.

"I realized Dolan was right," she said. "I did stumble across a needle in the haystack when I found a couple of solid suspects, but then I realized it wasn't me that did the stumbling. This all started in my spin class."

"Someone targeted her." Dolan added.

Ellie looked between the two, finding it hard not to smile.

"What?" Dolan asked.

"You're working together." Ellie hugged herself, pleased that the two people she loved the most in the world weren't arguing anymore. "How did that happen?"

"Anyway," Paisley skipped over that small detail, "once Dolan and I compared notes, we knew it was a setup."

"I got Mrs. Newton to corroborate Paisley's theory that Rachel was helping her collect evidence for the divorce." Dolan tipped his head in Paisley's direction. "However you found out about those divorce files, I don't want to know, but thank you."

"You're welcome," Ellie said.

Paisley nodded. "Yes, Ellie deserves all the credit on that score."

"So, Mrs. Newton killed her husband?" Ellie asked, trying to jump ahead.

"No," Paisley said, bluntly. "But when you found that full bottle of Linger perfume, it was obvious to me that Rachel might have had second thoughts about skewering Mr. Newton with divorce papers. What if she thought there was a chance to rekindle things with Newton, so she bought the perfume to signal her intentions when they met at my class?"

"So... Mrs. Newton killed Rachel?" Ellie looked confused.

"No," Paisley said it gently this time. "We think someone tried to capitalize on Rachel's momentary weakness, since she was clearly over Mr. Newton the next day on the hike."

"Someone wanted those divorce files," Dolan took over the story, "but Newton was all upset at Paisley's class. Maybe he wasn't mad at Paisley, but mad at Rachel for showing up."

"And why would someone want to make Newton mad?" Paisley asked Dolan, knowing the answer and setting up their big revelation.

"They wanted Newton all worked up so we'd blame his death on natural causes—namely—his emotional state and Paisley's spin class."

"Who? Why?" Ellie asked, sitting on the edge of the bed.

"We don't know for sure," Paisley admitted, "but our theory is that someone didn't want the Newtons to divorce."

"Do they have kids?" Ellie considered all the potential suspects, then something dawned on her. "When did you two get together and figure all this out?"

"Early this morning," Paisley said, "when you were sleeping."

Eyebrows rose, but Ellie didn't dig for details.

"Don't read anything into this," Dolan said, downplaying their collaboration. "I just couldn't keep avoiding the fact that Paisley has a way of finding things out. Even when I tell her not to interfere."

"Luckily, as a U.S. Marshal, Dolan's smarter than a mere man," Paisley said, countering him tit for tat, although it made her frown.

"And I was afraid you'd never get along," Ellie said.

"We're fine." Dolan cleared his throat. "But your part—both of yours—is over."

"Over?" Paisley questioned. "I plan to see this all the way through. I'm the bait."

Dolan laughed. "I never agreed to that."

"Then who did you think would trot around with the copy of our fake files, which we should say are on a thumb drive. I have one somewhere." She turned away to search for it in her purse.

He snorted, finally realizing Paisley was serious. "A police woman will be the bait."

Paisley didn't know what to say.

Jumping into the fray, Ellie grasped at the brief harmony they'd shown. "Oh, well, misunderstandings happen. It makes total sense to let the authorities handle it from here, don't you think, Paisley?"

She didn't answer.

Dolan faced her. "Of course, she agrees. A female officer will be here tonight. "

"She better look just like me."

"I would never put you in a dangerous spot like that!" Dolan was adamant. "There are too many uncontrollable variables."

"He's right," Ellie agreed, quickly backing down when she saw Paisley's devastated expression. "However, we certainly have enough personnel between the U.S. Marshals and the local officers to set a safe trap. Don't we?"

Dolan shook his head. "You change sides fast."

"I see both sides. It's a curse." Ellie bit her lip. "You know, acting as bait for a killer is not without danger, but you'd never find anyone that looks like Paisley. Do you want to catch this guy or not?"

Paisley held her breath, as if her whole world pivoted on his answer.

"Is there a response I can give you that all of us can live with?" Dolan paced, muttering to himself.

"It's not like the killer uses a gun," Paisley said. "How about this? Let's use the resort rumor mill to head him to the cafe's outdoor patio. It will be easy to stake out. Less people, wide open. If I get into trouble, I'll just run out to the boardwalk and expose the killer."

"We will run out to the boardwalk," Ellie said, standing up in a show of solidarity. "Two is safer than one."

"No way!" Dolan shouted. "I won't allow it." He recoiled at their expressions. "I can lock you in the bathroom."

"It locks on the inside," Ellie huffed.

Paisley had to do something quick, or he'd snatch the whole, glorious adventure right out from under her. "Dolan, take a minute to think about it. The killer's main weapon is a bath tub. I think we'll be safe on the patio."

"Safer than in here." Ellie looked over her shoulder at the tiny bathroom. It had a tub.

"We never found the chef's souped-up cattle prod. A shock from that would stop your heart." Dolan wouldn't hear of using them as bait.

Paisley and Ellie shared a look. "Don't decide just yet," Paisley advised. "When does the cafe close?"

"It's open late," Ellie quickly answered. "I think there's a night cap special that ends at midnight."

"Then we have until midnight, if we spread a rumor that I found the thumb drive and I'm going to sell it to Mrs. Newton at a midnight rendezvous."

"Will Mrs. Newton back that up?" Dolan wasn't so sure.

With a nod, Paisley assured him she would. "She'll do anything to wrap this up and get out of here."

Ellie raised her fists like little pompoms. "Sounds like a good plan, doesn't it?"

With a negative sounding groan, Dolan got up and headed for the door.

"What does that mean?" Paisley asked, following him.

"Nothing happens without approval. I certainly can't green light your crazy plan, especially since I don't like it." Without looking back, he grumbled, "I'll call you."

Chapter 8

Back to the Rusty Fig

The digital bedside clock clicked to show 11:45 p.m.

Paisley slid out of bed and quickly put on jeans when the lights suddenly turned on.

"Where are you going?" Ellie blinked, rubbing her eyes.

"Go back to sleep," Paisley ordered, as she skipped socks and slipped bare feet into tennis shoes.

"Did Dolan call?" Ellie asked. "Are we doing it?"

Paisley heaved a sigh. "I'm doing it. You're staying."

Ellie was already out of bed, pulling on jeans, as well. She struggled to get her pink night shirt off. "Forget that! You guys need to stop trying to protect me!"

"What are you doing?" Paisley asked, alarmed.

"I'm coming with you!"

The digital clock ticked to 11:48 p.m.

With a frustrated mutter, Paisley hurried out of their room to get to the patio cafe before it closed. Ellie chased right behind, half dressed and stumbling to get a shoe on.

"Go back to bed," Paisley hissed, keeping her voice low. The last thing she wanted to do was wake any guests.

"Make me!" Ellie challenged.

"I don't have the time!"

"I'll take that as a 'Please come with me, Ellie. I need your help!'" Ellie got her shoe on and caught up to Paisley. "You need me."

Bypassing the elevator for the stairs, Paisley held the door open for her friend. "Sure, one person meeting for a secret rendezvous is dangerous. Two makes it a garden party."

"Two, plus an overprotective brother and a bunch of police hiding in the bushes." She led the way down the stairs taking them two at a time.

Paisley hung back a minute, swallowing a confession. She knew she should admit the truth... Dolan never called or gave his approval. But she didn't.

Which brings us back to the that creepy night on the lake, where we first found the Fit Girls!

If you recall, they were dead in the water on the Rusty Fig.

A crackling sound snapped and sparked from the stranger's direction at the end of the dock. Ellie squinted in the darkness, unsure of the noise. "That sounds..." she started to say.

"...bad," Paisley finished. She recognized the sizzling snaps as the souped-up, missing cattle prod. "Water and electricity don't mix."

With a little prayer, she tried the ignition key again. "Please, please," Paisley coaxed.

The engine turned over.

Ellie took control of the steering. She backed the pontoon away from the dock. "Where to? I vote for far away from that!" She pointed at the crackling spark of the cattle prod in the killer's hands.

The shocks of light were the only thing on the dock clearly visible. Each spark lit up the air with thin, blinding streaks. They cast weird shadows that did nothing to reveal the killer's identity. If anything, the 'light show' only added to the murderer's mystique—only illuminating a grotesque grin.

Paisley focused on memorizing what could help her. She noted a strong chin, full lips, dark hair pulled back but not much else. It could be either one of two people. She considered shouting out a name. One lingered on the tip of her tongue...

...but the cattle prod sparks stopped.

Paisley went to the stern, the closest part of their boat to the shore. She strained to see.

"Did the killer give up?" Ellie asked from the opposite end of the boat.

Paisley felt, more than saw a figure move along the dock. It hopped into a boat and fired up the engine. "No, the killer is coming after us! Head to the boardwalk. We don't need the dock to get back to land. Just get us close enough to jump onto the boardwalk."

Ellie cranked the throttle all the way up and headed toward the boardwalk but at an angle away from the other boat, so it could not intercept them. The soft, romantic lights beckoned.

"What about Dolan? Did you reach him?" Paisley knew her actions were misguided, but she'd known he was still on the property and a quick call away.

"I only had time to send a 911. Oh no," Ellie groaned, looking at her phone. "I must have typed it wrong... I sent 411. I'll re-send."

Paisley knew the only fault was her own. They couldn't wait for Dolan. "Cut the engine." She'd put them in danger, so she'd get them out.

"What?" Ellie was certain she'd heard wrong.

"Turn it off. I want the killer to be able to hear me."

Ellie complied, but she didn't like it. She gunned the engine for just a second and cut it back, counting on the burst of power to add to their momentum. At the very least, it would keep them drifting toward the boardwalk.

"You don't have to do this," Paisley shouted to the other boat. She wasn't sure if her voice would carry over the expanse. The boat engines were electric, making them less noisy than their diesel counterparts but distance, added to the engine hum, made it hard to be heard.

The killer cutback the engine, too, but not completely off. The second boat began to close some of the distance between them.

"It's not like before," Paisley continued, believing her voice had to carry over the relatively smooth water. "You can't pin this on natural causes anymore, or on Rachel. The authorities are coming. It's all been a setup to flush you out. You should run. You don't know it yet, but you're trapped. It's over."

The killer laughed. The throaty chortle had an edge of madness to it, drifting across the water.

"Oh!" Ellie cried and started up the engine of their boat without needing to be told. They jerked forward, causing Paisley to stumble. She caught the railing, keeping herself from falling over... however, she could have sworn something moved just beneath the surface of the water. 'Probably just a wave, caused by the boats.' She didn't have the time—or enough light—to see if it was something else.

The killer had clearly heard enough and was coming for them. The second boat's engine throttled higher. It labored at max speed—which was pretty slow.

Paisley staggered to Ellie. "Stop the boat, again."

"Are you nuts?" Ellie had no intention of stopping. "We can reach the shore first."

Paisley kept her voice low, tone even. "Trust me. We need the other boat to get closer."

"Closer?" Ellie knew they were running out of time and distance to play games. Yet, she throttled back, allowing the killer's boat to gain on them again. "I hope you know what you're doing."

As the boats drew closer, Paisley went to the back of hers. She reached for a spotlight attached to the side for night fishing. She cranked it up and blasted the spot at their pursuer—exposing Felicity Lange at the wheel!

The light stunned the resort manager, causing her eyes to shut. When they opened, pure hatred stared back.

Paisley couldn't look away. The resort manager appeared possessed. She was nothing like the efficient boss Paisley had grown to know and respect. She gasped to Ellie, "Go, go, go! Start the engine!"

Revealing the killer might have been important, but it came with a huge consequence. Felicity had closed the distance between the boats. Plus, as they got closer to shore, she kept her throttle wide open, while Ellie wisely backed off. Even at a lesser speed, the pontoon boat would not stop on a dime.

"Brace yourself," Ellie warned.

"Felicity, it's over!" Paisley shouted, hoping against hope to get through to the woman.

"It's not over!" Felicity screamed. "Until you're gone!"

Paisley hurried to Ellie's side. They braced for impact.

"Whatever happens, just get yourself onto the boardwalk." Paisley told her friend.

"We'll get each other onto the boardwalk," Ellie corrected. "Right? We're in this together."

Paisley shook her head, mesmerized by the boardwalk's soft lights. They got closer and closer... moving far too fast. "Reverse the engines!"

Without questioning the order, Ellie obeyed. As their boat momentarily fought the forward momentum, churning water around the hull, Felicity's boat rammed into them from behind. The force threw Paisley to the deck. Ellie held tight to the steering controls and stayed on her feet.

The collision forced one of the pontoons from Felicity's boat to ride up on the other boat. It smashed them together, as if they were a new vessel. Felicity laughed, completely losing it. "Prepare to be boarded!"

The added push propelled the girls' boat onto the boardwalk. Wood splintered, as the bow crumbled under contact with the solid barrier. Water splashed and showered all around. The torturous collision echoed around the lake.

Engines whining with nowhere to go, as Paisley rolled onto her feet. She motioned for Ellie to escape. The wreckage made for a treacherous bridge to reach the boardwalk, but it would do. Ellie climbed over the boat's controls, standing on what was left of the bow of the ship. Her feet slipped on the slanted surface, but she got far enough to jump to shore... and into the waiting arms of Agnew!

"Are you okay?" he looked over her head, spotting Paisley.

"Help her!" Ellie gasped.

Other voices shouted, nearby. More help was coming, Paisley realized, if she couldn't fight her off long enough.

The angle of the boat, however made it hard to escape. Paisley slipped toward the stern's railing... and toward Felicity. The demented woman jumped across to the damaged boat, cattle prod in hand. She turned it on. A jolt of electricity shocked the air. It created a burning smell, even without coming into contact with human flesh. At least, Paisley thought she smelled something deadly.

"You couldn't leave it alone, could you?" Felicity stepped off her mangled pontoon onto Paisley's. "You'll live to regret that, but not for long."

Paisley tried to move, but slipped again. She managed to get to her feet, catching herself on a seating bench. It wrapped around the inside back of the boat. Beneath each cushioned section was storage and the engine. Out of pure instinct, Paisley grabbed a square-shaped cushion and hurdled it at Felicity like a flying disk.

It caught her by surprise and knocked the cattle prod out of her hands. The metal poll clattered onto the deck. The slant of the boat, however, made it slide right back to her feet. "You'll have to do better than that," Felicity challenged.

As she bent to pick up the cattle prod, Paisley stood and launched herself at the killer. The body check caused them to fall over the boat's railing into the other boat. The commotion rocked the boats, creating waves.

"Stop! I'll shoot!" Agnew ordered from his perch on the wrecked boat's bow.

"Don't!" Ellie shouted, behind him on the dock. Chef Armand, having cut across the landscaping, jumped onto the boardwalk to help. He moved around Ellie to put a hand on the wrecked pontoon. A piece of it broke off. He backed away, worried he would dislodge the craft. Agnew's weight was almost too much, as he moved farther onto the damaged vessel.

"Felicity, no!" Armand shouted.

Agnew fired a warning shot in the air.

It made Paisley flinch, but threats had no effect on the resort manager. Her focus was laser sharp. All she saw was her prey. Paisley wasn't even sure anything they said registered. Felicity's eyes were wild.

"Fight for your life!" Felicity ordered, as her voice lowered to an even deadlier whisper. "Or drown."

She lunged at Paisley, who stumbled backward, trying to get to the edge and jump back into the safety of her pontoon—closer to Agnew. However, she was dangerously close to falling into the lake, instead. Her movement jostled the vessels again, but something stronger churned the water between the boats. A wave forced them apart.

Paisley jumped with everything she had, spanning the gap between the vessels to land hard on the deck of her boat.

Felicity screamed, losing her balance on the rocking deck of her craft.

Agnew scrambled to Paisley's side, helping her up onto the slanted boat deck. He leveled his gun at Felicity, but the tortured woman ducked low, started her pontoon and backed away from them.

Paisley helplessly watched, as Felicity's boat disappeared into the darkness.

"Are you okay?" Agnew's hand cupped Paisley's chin, getting a good look at her eyes. "You're in shock."

Paisley pushed his hand aside. "We have to follow her."

He put his gun away. "She can't get far."

"Paisley!" Dolan shouted from the boardwalk. He hugged Ellie, before bracing a foot against the wreckage to reach out a hand for her.

Finally on the boardwalk, Paisley brushed aside everyone's concern. They'd have questions next, and eventually reproof for her lack of judgement. She had to circumvent all of that or the killer would get away. "Felicity Lange is the killer and she's on that boat!"

Dolan nodded at Agnew. "Is there another place to dock?"

"She could jump out and swim for the boardwalk at any point, but there's only one easy place to climb out." He pointed to a halfway spot at the far side of the lake. "There's a ladder to climb up to the boardwalk, and it's near a path that leads over the mountains."

"You can't let her escape!" Paisley wanted to join the search.

As more police officers arrived, Dolan directed them to follow him. The girls and Chef Armand would stay behind. "Agnew... get them up to the resort."

Relegated to a bodyguard, the trooper didn't like it, but followed his orders. "You can count on me, sir."

Without another word, Dolan ran off with his team to intercept Felicity before she could escape.

Chef Armand put his arm around Ellie's shoulder. "What a horrible turn of events for our serene home. At least you are safe, my sweet. Are you hungry?"

Ellie relaxed in his care. "I might need a little sugar."

"Your wish is my command!" He guided her up the path to the cafe patio. She briefly looked back at her friend and winked.

Paisley had no need for food. Frustrated and a little stunned that the whole thing was over, she paced. 'It's not fair!' she thought. 'Didn't I find the killer? Yes! But I'll miss the capture.' The only thing that consoled her was that Ellie was out of harms way.

"Do you think we could just walk around the boardwalk a little bit to see what's happening?" Paisley imagined getting close enough to see Dolan put Felicity in handcuffs.

"No," Agnew said. "I have other plans for you."

Paisley wasn't sure what he meant, until she turned to see his gun back in his hand.

"I really thought you'd buy Rachel's suicide." He sighed, making a little tsk-tsk sound, looking over Paisley's shoulder. "Guess you were right, sis."

Paisley spun around, stumbling back as Felicity climbed up onto the boardwalk from the lake. Dripping wet, her demonic look only intensified. She cocked her head to the side. "Miss me?"

Chapter 9

Everyone's in Trouble

"I jumped," Felicity explained, quite proud of herself. "I don't think your handsome U.S. Marshal will figure it out fast enough. My boat probably died in the middle of the lake. Wanna join it?"

Being an amateur sleuth had its downside, Paisley decided. Especially when confronted by a lunatic suspect and a suspect you never suspected. "No, Agnew, don't do this."

"I really liked you, too," he admitted. "Don't see that kind of determination very often, even if it turned out to be rather foolhardy. I tried to warn you against investigating further."

Thinking back, Paisley wasn't so sure. "Maybe you were just pumping me for information to see what I knew. What I discovered."

He nodded agreement. "You were definitely onto my sister."

"Didn't help you in the end, did it?" Felicity hunkered down a bit, spreading her arms wide as she moved forward, closing her snare. Each step she took made Paisley move away, but Agnew compensated. She was trapped between them.

Of course, she couldn't do anything to get away from the gun, but neither could Felicity, Paisley realized. She judged the position of the siblings. "Careful," she warned Agnew. "If you shoot me, you might hit your sister."

He smirked, practically challenging her to think it through.

"Unless... you want to shoot your sister?" Paisley read his expression as confirmation. If only she had time to make it work in her favor. "Don't you see, Felicity, he wants to shoot both of us. Maybe he's done cleaning up you messes? We're almost lined up perfectly for him to get both of us with one bullet."

"Stop talking!" Felicity lurched forward, trying to grab her around the neck in a chokehold.

Paisley got a hand under Felicity's arm, fighting the pressure. "You're making it too easy. Look!"

For the fist time, Felicity noticed her brother. His gun still pointed at Paisley. "Put it down. I got her."

Agnew shook his head. "Stop! Let her go!" he shouted.

"What are you doing?" Felicity snarled.

"He's setting the stage," Paisley whispered. "Help is coming and he's not going down with you."

Wild eyes darting about, Felicity finally saw the lights coming around the boardwalk.

Dolan and his team were heading back. They'd be on them in minutes.

"His only way out is to kill both of us!" Paisley struggled to get free, but Felicity only held her tighter.

"He's my family," Felicity hissed.

Agnew took a step closer, but he didn't lower the gun. He still had both of them in his sights.

Paisley screamed, but she couldn't get free.

"I'll be devastated that I killed you, Paisley," Agnew admitted, already conjuring up a tear. "Felicity wouldn't let you go. She was demented. I threatened her, but she started to choke you. Even your own tragic love, Dolan, will be my witness. He's close enough now to see me move in to pull you away." He took a step closer, as Paisley twisted in Felicity's grip. "But then the gun went off."

"No!" Felicity realized his intentions too late.

A gunshot echoed across the lake.

Instant commotion surrounded the area. Paisley fell to the boardwalk, as a splash signaled that someone had gone into the water. More splashes, but she souldn't see what was happening. She'd landed looking the other way. It all felt like slow motion, but she knew it had to be the shock. The sounds around her muted, even as she recognized the voices of people she loved.

'It's over,' she thought. 'I got my wish. I was here at the end.'

The fog cleared for a moment, as she breathed in fresh air. Someone pulled her to her feet, then picked her up in their arms. Dolan? She wanted to say something to him... but she spotted Agnew.

He'd slumped to his knees on the boardwalk, clutching his bloody gun hand. Serveral other troopers stood around him, looking rather grim. One of them yanked Agnew to his feet, none too gentle.

As the strong arms cradled her close, carrying her up the path to the resort, Paisley shifted to see the lake. More officers stood around a bedraggle, deflated Felicity. She moaned, crying for someone to listen. They put her in handcuffs.

By the time Dolan got her into the resort dining room, where a steaming pot of coffee and a brandy shot awaited, Paisley felt the shock fade. The world sped back up to normal.

"We never should have left you," Ellie wailed, ignoring her brother and hugging her friend still in his arms. Chef Armand stood nearby. He'd never left Ellie's side. "How could this happen?"

"Ellie, please," Dolan muttered.

She stepped back, and Dolan sat Paisley in a chair, kneeling next to her and rubbing her hands.

"They're brother and sister." Paisley heard the quiver in her voice and took a deep breath.

"When did you figure that out?" Dolan asked, as worry and quilt wrinkled his brow.

"A bit too late, I'm afraid." Paisley shook her head, and gently pulled one hand away from Dolan. She reached for the brandy.

"Easy," he said, noticing her hand shake.

She sipped the liquid medicine, instantly feeling the burn. It calmed her nerves. "What happened there at the end?" she asked. "I think I missed the best part."

Ellie gave a nervous laugh. "Oh, I think you were right in the thick of it."

"We saw it all from the patio," Chef Armand admitted. "A terrible, terrible thing to be so close, yet too far away to help."

"Dolan got there in time," Ellie said, proud of her brother.

Paisley squeezed his hand, as Dolan pulled a chair close and sat next to her. "Well, I got within shooting distance."

"You were the one that fired a gun?" Paisley had been certain it was Agnew.

"He shot that slimy Agnew's gun right out of his hand before he could hurt you!" Ellie interjected, beaming.

Dolan almost blushed. "Just doing my job, ma'am."

"Which job?" Ellie asked, a twinkle of mischief in her eyes. "As a U.S. Marshal or an ex-fiance?"

Paisley sighed, relieved that the whole thing was over. "To Dolan!" She toasted him and drank the rest of the brandy in one gulp.

Rubbing the side of his face, feeling the stubble that had popped up, Dolan accepted her thanks. A little of his worry faded. "Another round," he ordered. "I feel like celebrating."

Justice moved pretty fast, once Trooper Agnew and Felicity Agnew Lange were in custody. She'd dropped her maiden name long ago, making it understandable why no one connected the dots. In their separate confessions, they blamed each other. Each claimed that their love of the area and wanting to protect its good name played in their motives. The catalyst, however, had been Mr. Newton's upcoming divorce. Felicity knew it would expose her complicity.

"I don't know," Dolan admitted to Paisley, as she walked him out the main entrance of the Grand Teton Bluebird Resort. "Seems to me less murder would have protected the area's reputation better."

The resort, however, had not suffered. The murders and arrests brought in media and guests looking for a little excitement with their massages and fine dining. Paisley and Dolan had to weave through several vehicles blocking the circular drive, unloading guests. Luckily, Dolan had found a place to park upfront. He put his gear in the trunk.

"From what I heard, but have not been able to confirm," Paisley said, bitting her lip, hoping it didn't sound like she was fishing for information, although she was, "Agnew killed Rachel when they discovered she'd be a witness in the divorce trial; and Felicity killed Mr. Newton because the trial would have exposed her part in all his torrid affairs."

Dolan nodded, considering the rumors. "And what part would that be?"

"Well, I spoke to Mrs. Newton, and she thought Felicity had made most of the introductions between Mr. Newton and his ladies, for a generous tip. Not a fact that would get her a promotion. She would have probably been fired."

"As rumors go, that's a good one." Dolan did little to confirm or deny.

She nudged him in the arm. "Come on, you can tell me."

"I thought you'd be done with investigating."

Ignoring the suggestion, Paisley pressed on with her theories. "I also spoke to Marika. She really did love Mr. Newton, and they'd rekindled their affair. He was giving up all the other women, including his wife, for her. Marika said he wasn't going to fight the divorce—and even planned to admit to his many liaisons—as a way to make amends to Mrs. Newton. He was ready to come clean."

"Yeah, right. You're too kind and Marika's living a fantasy. Men like that don't change," Dolan said, not willing to give Mr. Newton the benefit of the doubt.

"I guess we'll never know if he would have gone through with it," Paisley said, lost in what could have been, if only Mr. Newton been a better man.

"Well, Felicity believed it, so maybe you're right," Dolan pointed out. "Of course, she had too much at risk not to believe. On top of his divorce exposing her, she'd grown to regret being one of his many conquests. Or so she said."

Paisley couldn't help but hug his arm. "Thanks for sharing all the details with me."

"I was afraid you'd break into my office just to read the official report." He shut the trunk lid, ready to go. He just wasn't ready to say goodbye.

"What about Agnew?" Paisley sucked in a breath. She'd avoided asking about him but couldn't any longer. "There are so many other choices he could have made."

Dolan shrugged. "Sometimes, women can make you do crazy things. Even if she's just your sister."

He turned back to the resort entrance and waved. Ellie waited there, clever enough to give them a moment alone. As she put it... she wanted none of their 'adult talk.'

"What about you and Ellie?" He nodded toward his sister.

Paisley pivoted to look at her friend, before turning back to Dolan. "I need to finish out my time at the Bluebird, but we want to travel. Luckily, I have more offers for work.

I promise I'll do a better job of taking care of your sister. No more putting Ellie in danger."

"Don't make a promise you can't keep." He turned toward the driver side door, but thought better of it. He walked back to her, getting a little too close for Paisley's comfort.

She steeled herself for his parting words... or actions.

"I know you're done talking about this thing that happened between us, but I'm not." Dolan ran a hand through his hair.

Paisley sighed. She liked him confused, even though it gave her hope when she was ready to move on. "Just boil it down to one word, agent."

"Fear." Dolan owned it, looking her straight in the eyes.

"I accept your apology," Paisley said, realizing it was the best thing for both of them.

"I was apologizing?" Dolan stepped back. He clearly did not think he was apologizing.

Paisley let her eyes look past him, hoping to see someone ready to interrupt. Maybe a valet, or a straggling trooper? 'Where were all the police officers when you needed one?' she silently wondered. 'Didn't they want to shake the U.S. Marshal's hand or something?' Unfortunately, they were pretty much alone.

"I was trying to get us talking," Dolan admitted. "Doesn't talking sound better than apologizing?"

"No, because I apologize, too," Paisley said.

He didn't know what to make of it. Confusion settled on his shoulders. "You? That's a twist."

Taking a deep breath, Paisley let it go... with the truth she'd been avoiding since she ran away to the Grand Teton Bluebird Resort. "I left you at the altar, too."

"What?" Dolan's casual, cocky 'I can handle anything' exterior crumbled.

"I went to the church, but I didn't put on the wedding dress." Paisley found it easy, after all, to tell him her side of their 'almost' wedding day. He was the only one that needed to know, outside of Ellie who'd figured it out on her own. "When they came to tell me about you—to give me your note—no one noticed that I wasn't ready. But I wasn't. And I wasn't going to get ready."

The birds chirped, a hawk flew overhead. Nothing around them signaled a momentous moment. Dolan just shook his head, slowly understanding. "Why weren't you getting ready?"

"It didn't feel like my wedding day." There it was... the truth. She didn't want to get married any more than Dolan.

Dolan clapped his hands together. "So we're even!"

She let him have one, relieved to have the truth out. Secrets never stayed secrets for long.

"Well, I was going to let you down in person." She let that sink in, canceling any thoughts he had of doing a happy dance.

U.S. Marshal Dolan Cruz knew how to take a setback. He nodded, fully getting the difference between running away from a problem and facing it head-on. "So, we're almost even."

Paisley gave him a quick wink. "We're almost a lot of things."

"Felicity named the boats?" Ellie shook her head at the clue that had evaded them. It took gossiping with a handy man to figure it out, well after all the mystery.

"Let's not talk about her anymore," Paisley pleaded. "I feel like we've been on a loop, forever talking about what happened. I'm ready for a new adventure."

With the car loaded, healthy snacks and plenty of water in a back seat cooler, the girls waved goodbye to the Grand Teton Bluebird Resort. It didn't feel like running away this time. The owners had asked Paisley to stay on after her three-month contract ended. They liked having someone on property intimately familiar with the recent, notorious events. The sensational headlines, as it turned out, drew tourists hungry for all the deadly details.

The regular Bluebird clientele had left for their vacation homes, wanting to avoid any scent of scandal. Getting caught up in the tragedy wasn't for Paisley, either, although she was offered a generous salary bump. Instead, she accepted a short gig at an exclusive mansion estate. It promised the excitement of a wedding, hidden away in the flatlands of Indiana.

"I'm over Felicity, too, but I think we still have a mystery to solve," Ellie stated, plugging her cell phone into the car's radio. One of her favorite indy rock tunes exploded from the car's speakers.

Paisley didn't take the bait, as she turned down the volume.

"The Lake Monster." Ellie bopped her head from side to side. "What do they call him?"

"The Teton Tease," Paisley supplied.

"I think the Teton Tease un-stuck our boat from Felicity's. He kinda saved us."

Paisley shook her head, not accepting the explanation. "Plenty of other things could have caused the boats to separate."

"I don't know," Ellie said, warming to the idea. "If Felicity and Agnew were trying to save the resort's good name, maybe the Lake Monster was too. I don't think he liked them."

Paisley reached for her sunglasses, tucked into the visor. "Interesting, but I'd rather find a different kind of adventure than taking on local folklore."

"Hope it's a small adventure with new, cute men," Ellie sighed. She already missed Chef Armand.

"It's a mansion, how small can it really be?" Paisley asked. "Besides, less people means we'll really get to know my clients."

"Bridesmaids? I'm not so sure they'll be fun, especially if they have to lose weight to fit into their dresses." Ellie relaxed in her seat. "You'll have your hands full of cranky, bloated women."

"Don't worry. I have a good feeling about the Childress Estate." Paisley had already read up on their new location. "It's part of an adorable small town, with great little shops and wonderful restaurants. There's even a nearby Amish community."

Ellie sighed, resigned to starting all over again with new people and new healthy food to endure. "As your trip deejay, I am open to suggestions. More of my jamming tunes or would you like to listen to a local station?"

"How about nothing?" Paisley liked the sound of the wheels on the road. They sounded hopeful to her... hope of seeing more of the world and figuring her place in it.

Ellie turned the music off.

If they had turned to a local radio station, though, they would have heard a news report about Felicity Agnew Lange escaping from jail.

The End

About Fit Girls

Every book in the Fit Girls Series is a
short read, which means they are a novella
length and that also makes them perfect
for the Large Print format, because they
aren't crazy thick books but they are still a
complete mystery, with a beginning, middle
and end. The main characters carry over
to the next story, but each book is one
mystery. You can read them in any order. If
there's something you should know about
the characters from prior books, it will be
included. Just be assured that every book is
a full story about the mysteries that arise
as the main character, Paisley Summerhill,
travels for work. She's a fitness instructor
working short, special fitness gigs at fancy

resorts and exotic locations, all around the world.

The Fit Girl Series in Large Print format:

Book #1 - Fit Girls: Exercise is Murder

Book #2 - Fit Girls: Weddings are Murder

Book #3 - Fit Girls: Pet Shows are Murder

Book #4 – Fit Girls: Trains are Murder